WHERE YOU LIVE

By Gary McMahon

Published by Crystal Lake Publishing
www.CrystallakePub.com

Edited by Joe Mynhardt

Content:

It Knows Where You Live

Other Monsters

Acknowledgments:

Thanks to Gary Fry for publishing the original edition; to Joe Mynhardt for agreeing to publish it again – along with the other stories, of course; and finally, as always, to my beloved Charlie and Emily for being where I live.

Dedication:

To Second Chances

Author's Foreword:

It's just about morning here: coffee and yawning; that weird empty lull before sunrise. I have to write this brief introduction, but I'm tired and distracted. I'll try my best, but forgive me if some of the minor details are incorrect.

Back in 2012 a collection of mine called **It Knows Where You Live** was published as a signed, limited hardback by Gray Friar Press. The subtitle of the book was "modern tales of unease". That didn't make it into the printed book, but it exists in the Word file. Only one hundred copies of the book were ever printed. I inscribed a small, unique message in each one. It's a gorgeous little volume. The print run sold out before it was even produced.

Ever since then, people have continually asked me if I have any spare copies. The book was in-demand, but there were no copies remaining – even the book dealers sold out fast. I always thought we missed a trick not putting out a trade paperback edition. Now, especially with the popularity of eBooks, it seems like the right time to make the book available again…but in a slightly different form. When I contacted Joe at Crystal Lake Publishing and pitched him the idea, I was delighted he seemed keen to run with it. I've worked with Joe before; he's a good guy. I like working with good people.

This new edition leaves out three stories from the original hardback: *Among the Leftovers*, *Hope is a Small Thing Dying in a Bin Behind an Abandoned Kebab Shop*, and *Nine Lives*. I left these stories out for two reasons: one, to ensure those who bought the original hardback didn't feel cheated; and, two, because I wanted to streamline the first part of this book to make room for the additional material. I think they're good stories, but they're short, and their absence doesn't affect the flow of the book.

The additional material I mentioned (subtitled "Other Monsters") consists of two obscure reprints and five brand new pieces of fiction. I wanted to make this book attractive enough to whoever bought the original that they might consider putting their hands in their pockets again. I don't want to cheat people. I'll leave the cheating to others.

So, welcome to where I live, the fictional world I inhabit. It's cold and dark, but hope still blooms in the shadows. You just have to look hard enough, and with the right kind of eyes. Sometimes fantasy and reality tend to blur; the lines between those two states get fuzzy.

Strange things can happen here. Things nice people don't like to talk about, but people like you and I love to discuss. In fact, let me tell you about something that happened only last night…

#

I told myself it would be a bit of fun: hiding beneath my son's bed, dressed up in a cheap clown suit and fright-wig, with my face covered in white greasepaint makeup. He'd get the shock of his life, and we'd laugh about it. Of course we would. We hadn't shared a joke in months, and everyone says laughter is food for the soul.

He doesn't get to laugh much since his mum left us, so I figured it would be good for him. Good for me, too, if I'm honest.

So I slid in under the bed frame, pushing aside the

discarded toys and torn magazines, and made myself comfortable down there – well, as comfortable as I could.

Then I waited. I waited to play my little joke.

Time passed. I wondered what was taking him so long to come upstairs. Surely he'd brushed his teeth by now? I waited and I waited and I think I fell asleep, just for a moment, or maybe a little longer. Whatever.

When I opened my eyes again, it was darker under the bed than it had been before. The room felt...*different*. I couldn't say how, it just did. Nothing felt the same.

I heard movement above me. The mattress creaked, the bed frame shuddered, and somebody was breathing softly. He was in bed. The little so-and-so. He must have come upstairs while I was dozing, slipping softly under the covers while I lay below. Perhaps he even knew I was there, under the bed, and was playing his own little joke. Turning the prank on the prankster.

Oh, how we'd laugh at that. We'd laugh and laugh until our faces ached.

Slowly, I began to edge sideways, moving out from under the bed. I was as quiet as a mouse, as soft as a promise. I straightened my back and got up onto my knees, rising slowly at the side of the bed with my hands grasping the edge of the bedclothes. Then I looked, preparing a smile.

"Hello, Daddy," said the scrawny yellow thing sitting on my son's bed, in a quavering, high-pitched voice. Its lidless eyes were as deep as the ocean and its wide mouth was filled with glinting silver. "I've been waiting for you." It lifted its bald, flabby head off the pillow, smiling through razorblades, long tongue hanging down onto its quivering, scaly chest.

Only then did I realise the joke was on me.

#

See what I mean?

I'm sure it happened, but this morning I woke up safe and sound in my bed. I felt a bit groggy, as if I had a hangover, but I was unharmed. I have no recollection of going to sleep.

When I finish typing this and email it to my publisher, I'll go to my son's room to wake him up for school. Part of me has been hanging back, scared of what I might find in there – because strange things have been known to happen where I live.

But none of this is your concern. It needn't bother you. Just have a read of the stories and enjoy them. They're only fictions: they can't really touch you, not where you are. Fear and dread cannot possibly bleed through the pages of a book.

Meanwhile, I'm off to check on my son.

I'll try to let you know how I get on.

Gary McMahon
Yorkshire
2013

It Knows Where You Live…

Just Another Horror Story

It begins with a man and a woman in a room. It always begins this way; has done since time immemorial. A couple, a pair of lovers on a bed in a single room, sprawled across the mattress, their bodies still slick with sweat from a bout of lovemaking. Words of passion still tremble on their lips like hummingbird wings. The lights are low. All is silent. Then, abruptly, one of them speaks...

#

"I remember hearing about something that happened here once. Or maybe I read it in a book – a book of real-life horror stories." Terry rolled onto his side and bent his elbow on the hard mattress, one hand supporting his chin and the other cupping his balls. He blinked in the darkness and looked at the woman by his side. "Something about a murder."

"Don't," said Nancy, but she was smiling, enjoying the game as it began. Her eyes glittered like rain on a pavement, reflecting the light from the main road outside the hotel window. They had left the blinds open even though it was a ground floor room. The window was guarded by a row of bushes, then the retaining wall of the car park. The main road was beyond, distant enough not to risk them being seen by anyone passing by.

"Go on," she said, warming to his theme, her eagerness negating the doubt she'd expressed in her previous statement.

Terry smiled. She thought his teeth looked too white –

like scrubbed fangs – in the darkness.

"There's this couple, right." He slithered on the bed. The springs creaked, adding a sound effect to his story. "They're illicit lovers, two married people meeting up to fuck." He paused.

She shook her head. "Yeah, yeah, yeah...I know: just like us."

He nodded. "So they've just been having sex and she goes for a shower." His gaze darted momentarily towards the bathroom. "He stays in the bed, thinking about joining her but too lazy to move. His eyes roam over the cheap hotel furniture and then up across the wall. That's when he sees it."

She was fumbling for the whisky bottle on the bedside cabinet. There was half left. She poured two glasses and handed one to him. He reached for it with his ball-fondling hand.

"What did he see?" Her voice was low, almost forlorn. She knew how this would end – if not the specifics, then the general outcome.

"There's this small hole on the wall, like a drill hole. Perfectly round, but with the wallpaper torn all around its edges. That's how he spots it: because of the torn paper.

He paused to take a drink.

She did the same, and grimaced. The whisky was raw, a crude blend, and the only glasses they'd been able to find in the petrol station shop were cheap dessert glasses.

"So he gets up and pads naked across the room. Staring at the little hole. He sees something glinting there, like glass catching the light from a passing car. When he gets really close, with his nose touching the wall, he sees it's a camera lens."

Nancy choked a little on her drink. "A camera?"

Terry nodded. "A camera."

She laughed softly. "Continue. Please. This is fascinating." But despite her sarcasm she did feel a sudden chill, the stipple of gooseflesh across her bare arms.

"So she's still in the shower. He leaves the room and stands outside the door to the next room – the one where he thinks the camera must be located." He paused again, drank. "*That* room." He raised the glass and tilted it slightly towards the wall, indicating the room beyond.

"This wallpaper's terrible. Like something out of a 1970s porn flick." She pulled up the covers, trying to get warm again.

"Funny you should mention that…about a movie, I mean. The guy, our guy, he tries the door. It's unlocked. So he opens it and steps inside. There's the camera, pushed up against the wall with the business end of its lens pressed right against the hole. A black and white TV on the side shows the empty room he's just left, with the open bathroom door and steam from the shower creeping around the frame like a mist."

The traffic sounds from outside the window hit a lull, and the silence became deep and unfathomable. Terry took another drink, almost draining his glass. She could see that he was drunk; his bottom lip had gone soft and his eyes had taken on a familiar glaze.

"And," she said, knowing she would regret this later.

"And as he watches the other room on the small black and white screen he sees a masked figure, all done up in a leather gimp outfit, walk out of the bathroom holding his girlfriend's cut-off head in one hand. There's blood on her face and in her hair, and blood and stuff on the knife the

3

gimp has in his other hand."

She felt her body twitch and hated herself for it. She should have seen this coming – in fact, she had, or something very similar. Terry's stories always ended in blood and death.

"Then what?" she whispered.

"Then the figure steps sideways, moving away from the camera lens…and a few seconds later our guy hears the sound of the door as it clicks shut behind him."

The silence in the room seemed to stir, wrapping itself around them on the bed, and then Terry broke the spell by laughing.

"Bastard," she said, feeling disproportionately angry. She slid out of bed and walked towards the wall, right to the spot where he'd said there was a hole. Standing there naked, with the cool air caressing her buttocks, she groped across the wall with her fingertips. "There's nothing here," she said, more to herself than to him. "There isn't a hole, or a camera."

Terry was still laughing when she turned around, but when he saw her from the front – the breasts she knew always drew stares, the neatly trimmed patch between her smooth, gym-honed thighs – he suddenly stopped laughing.

She smiled, leaning her weight on her left leg. A flattering pose.

"Come here," he said, drawing back the covers to expose his erection. "Daddy wants to play."

She smiled despite her misgivings, forgetting the previous chill and the fact that the sadistic bastard enjoyed frightening her so much. Then, throwing back her head and adopting a faux catwalk strut, she went over to the bed and joined him, joined *with* him, forgetting about the silliness from earlier.

#

She woke much later, or that was how it felt. Darkness pressed against her face like a vast silken sheet. The window blind was closed; one of them, perhaps even she, must have closed it on a toilet run during the night. Her head felt big and heavy; a hangover was perched just over the rim of her skull. Her body ached from all the fucking and she felt clammy, as if she'd retained a layer of dried sweat over her skin.

"Terry…" She nudged him, jamming her elbow into his ribs, but he didn't move. He did not even make a sound. "I'm hungry." Nothing: he slept on, or pretended to.

She slipped out of bed and crossed the room, fumbling around on the floor for her clothes. She didn't want to turn on the light – not even one of the small lamps – in case she woke him. They had their friction, their silly little arguments, but deep down she thought she loved him more than anyone. Certainly more than her weak-willed husband, or the many lovers she'd taken prior to their hasty marriage.

She pulled on her jeans without putting on her knickers, and then slid her sweater over her head without bothering to even look for her bra. Her shoes were here somewhere. She remembered kicking them off. Over there: by the chair against the wall. She slipped her feet into the backless pumps and glanced back over her shoulder at Terry.

He lay there like a corpse. He wasn't even snoring. *Drunk as a skunk*, she thought. There was a book on the bed, a small hardback volume. She'd not noticed it before, when she got up, but now she spotted it immediately. She couldn't remember Terry bringing a book; he rarely even read magazines, let alone novels. She was the reader, the prose addict, in their furtive relationship. Maybe the book had been left behind by a previous tenant, and Terry had been browsing through it during the night, unable to sleep.

She walked over to the bed and picked up the book. **Horror Stories,** it said on the faded red cover. No illustration, just a bare cardboard frontage. No author or editor's name. Just the title: two words in black, a hackneyed phrase. The same words were repeated in the same workmanlike font along the cracked spine of the book.

Nancy turned over the book in her hands. The back cover was blank: no blurb, no cover quotes from other authors. It felt like a cheap binding: pulped card, rough to the touch. She turned the book back over, looking again at the cover.

Horror Stories

Her fingers played across the cover, but she was afraid to open it up and take a look. This reaction puzzled her. It made her feel like things had been taken out of her hands and she was unable to dictate her own actions.

She glanced over at Terry. He was lying on his right side, facing away from her. His head was a dark blur; his left arm was a lump attached to his side. It could have been anyone there, in the bed. Even a stranger.

Her gaze returned to the book in her hands. She wanted to throw it away, hurl it through the window and out into the night…instead, she put it back down on the bed, where she'd found it. Next to Terry's apparently sleeping form.

"Hungry," she said into the room, hoping there was no one else to hear. A soft rumbling in her stomach was the only response she received.

She turned and headed towards the room's door, and then at the last minute she veered sideways and returned to the spot on the wall that had featured in Terry's story. Her hands crawled across the smooth, dry wallpaper, looking for a hole, or perhaps a tear in the surface. She found nothing: just the skin of the paper and the lumpy wall beneath. She shook her head, feeling stupid for thinking of the story now, in the dark, and believing it might contain even a kernel of truth.

She went back over to the bed, and in an act of defiance she picked up the book and opened it to the first page. The paper was blank: no publishing history, no printer's name, and no list of acknowledgements. She turned to the next page, where she expected to find a table of contents, and saw yet another empty page. The paper looked cheap: it was rough to the touch and she could see the shape of the pulp.

She turned another page, and found the first, untitled story. The opening line – a snatch of dialogue – made her take a step back, keeping the book at arm's length:

"'I remember hearing about something that happened here once.'"

They were Terry's words, the ones he'd started his story with. She couldn't be certain if they were the *exact* words, of course – her memory wasn't good. But she was pretty sure that he'd used a phrase very much like the one she'd just read.

She closed the book, hard, slamming the covers shut. Then she placed the book carefully on the bed, but not too close to Terry, not this time…Why? In case the book was harmful?

It was like a dream had bled into waking life. None of this seemed entirely real, but it felt real enough to make her afraid. "Terry?"

Again, there was no response. She knew she could reach out, shake him awake, but for some reason she didn't want to make a move. *What if he doesn't wake up?* The thought, along with everything it implied, was simply too terrifying to contemplate.

She walked backwards, staring at the bed, the book – but not at Terry. Then, when she brushed against the chair with her thigh, she turned around and reached for the door handle. She opened the door. The landing outside was quiet and empty. Light spilled through the window at the end, the one situated near the staircase. She listened, but there was nothing much to be heard. Night noises; sleep sounds; the whispers of a building at rest.

She closed the door. Then she opened it again, but slowly this time. What was it she had noticed? The thing that had disturbed her yet intrigued her enough to look back out there.

She turned her head to the side. Yes, that was it: the door to the room next to theirs was open. She hadn't seen it – not exactly – but she must have sensed it, like a disturbance in the natural order of things. And the story – Terry's story; the one she'd seen at least partly retold in that book – was still fresh in her mind.

She'd read the stories and seen the movies. A woman roaming a darkened building, walking around and poking her nose into rooms she should have ignored. Acting silly, like a victim-in-waiting, as if she were deliberately looking to be hacked or slashed or beaten...

Yes, she knew all the stories by heart, but still she stepped out onto the landing and turned to face the partially open door. Blackness showed at the edge of the frame. She reached out a hand and pushed, gently, almost hesitantly, and the door opened further: the darkness at the edge grew wider.

"Hello. Is anyone in there?" Again, she felt silly saying the words, but it was all just part of the plot, an element of the story someone else had written. Why did she feel this way, as if her actions were being determined by another? Was it because the situation was so familiar from all the old stories and the scary films she'd ever seen?

"Don't be stupid," she said, answering her own question. "It's just an empty room. You know that." And she did; she knew it very well. Terry had asked when they checked into the hotel if there was anyone in the room next door. They both made a lot of noise during sex, and he didn't want to disturb anyone. The receptionist had blushed at his audacity, and then regained her composure, the professional mask slipping back into place. *No*, she'd said. *The room next to yours is empty. There's nobody staying there.*

Nancy pushed open the door. The room beyond was still and dim and not unlike their own. Light from the corridor illuminated the interior, not a lot, but just enough for her to see what was inside: a double bed, a wardrobe, a rickety chair by the door. Another door, this one closed to the frame, which must lead to the bathroom. A pile of books on the bed. A camera set up on a tripod against the adjoining wall.

Something flickered inside her head, like a faulty light

9

bulb. Her thoughts went dark.

She was caught in a moment, stuck between two different reactions: should she backtrack and return to their room, and confront the possibility of Terry's deep sleep not being sleep at all, or should she push on into this new room, this new situation, and face whatever was waiting for her?

She found herself stepping across the threshold, moving into the room. She made her way to the bed, and before she'd even picked up a single book she knew what she'd see on the cover. Two words; a hackneyed phrase:

Horror Stories

She picked up one, two books. They were identical…and exactly the same as the one she'd found in the other room, on the bed, next to her motionless lover. She opened one of the books and found it filled with blank pages. The next one was the same. And the next, the next, along with the several others she tried after that…perhaps a hundred copies of the same book, all filled with empty pages. She couldn't remember there being that many books when she'd first seen them.

She turned away from the bed and focused her attention on the camera. She knew nothing of this kind of technology, but it didn't look current. It wasn't digital. It was hooked up to a video recorder on top of a small television she had initially failed to see because it was on the floor, with its screen turned to face the wall.

Recalling the specifics of Terry's scare-story, she moved closer to the camera, trying not to touch it, not to brush against the legs of its tripod. The end of the lens was pressed right up against a small hole in the wall. She backed away, feeling a rush of panic. Then, recovering herself, she crouched down and turned the television set around so she could see its screen.

She glanced over her shoulder, at the door, and there was nobody out there on the landing. She was still alone. There was no threat here. This whole scene possessed the quality of an art installation: lots of attention to detail, a sense that somebody had arranged things in a certain way to evoke a specific emotional response.

On the television screen she could see the bed in the other room, and the shape of Terry on the mattress. The image was grainy, like CCTV footage, and it flickered constantly. She watched as a woman she knew to be herself entered the shot. The woman – this other Nancy – stood over the bed and picked up the book. She opened the book and looked at the pages. It was impossible to tell if they were blank or if anything was written on them. It was like a time-lapse image, a delayed recording of events she'd already lived through, things she had already done.

And then everything changed.

The woman began to read aloud, facing the bed, as if she were reciting a bedtime story to the man who was lying there, so unmoving. There was no sound; hers was a silent performance. The window blind was closed. The darkness in the room seemed to stir, but that could have been a result of the constant flickering of the image on the screen.

Nancy was no longer afraid. None of this felt real or solid. It was just another horror story, but one she was now part of. She stood up straight and walked across the room, casting one final glance at the pile of books on the bed. This time the books were all open to the first page, and there were regular lines of cramped text covering the paper. She didn't pause to read them; she just continued on her way, out of the room, onto the landing. To her right, where the staircase had been, there was now a wall of books – a dusty red hardbound barrier stretching from floor to ceiling, each component of which had the same three words printed along its spine.

She turned left, away from the overwhelming sight, and walked into the other room.

Terry was still on the bed, but the other woman – the alternative Nancy – was no longer there. She had left behind her copy of the book.

Horror Stories

Nancy approached the bed and picked up the book. She opened it to the inaugural story, the one without a title. The opening lines had changed from those she'd seen before, when she had first discovered the book. She began to read the prologue out loud:

"It begins with a man and a woman in a room. It always begins this way; has done since time immemorial. A couple, a pair of lovers on a bed in a single room, sprawled across the mattress, their bodies still slick with sweat from a bout of lovemaking. Words of passion still tremble on their lips like hummingbird wings. The lights are low. All is silent. Then, abruptly, one of them speaks…"

Below her, curled up on the bed where Terry should have been, something with a strange, muffled voice began to read along with her.

It was quiet when Berger got off the phone. He sat at the dining table, his hand still clutching the receiver even though he'd replaced it in its cradle, and stared at the wall. The wall that was part of his house: the same house that would soon belong to the mortgage company unless he managed to think of a solution fast.

The woman on the phone had been polite, even friendly, but the message she relayed was terrible: pay your outstanding mortgage or we'll repossess the property. Berger had been expecting the conversation for weeks – had even been putting it off because he was unable to face it. But now it was out of the way he felt strangely liberated, as if a handful of unseen tethers had been disconnected from his body. The sensation did not last; within seconds he felt once again encumbered, tied down by the weight of his responsibilities. Freedom, he thought, was a perishable illusion.

He glanced sideways, out of the window and into the garden. At first he thought there was a woman standing out there on the lawn, her body leaning at an odd angle, and then he realised it was merely a reflection of his wife in the glass. The sight triggered something in his mind; a memory of a dream he might once have had. Then this illusion – like so many others – dissolved.

"Tell me we won't lose the house."

Sophie stood behind him, framed by the kitchen doorway. He could not be sure how much of the conversation she had overheard, so decided to be honest. "I promise you I'll do everything I can to prevent it."

She moved towards him, her arms going around his shoulders from behind. The skin of her hands was cold against his cheek; her thin fingers rubbed at his stubble as if struggling to break through and touch him deep inside. "I know you will. You've never let us down."

He wished he could cry, but that wasn't the kind of man he aspired to be. He'd been trained to keep everything locked down inside, to swallow the pain and soldier on. Even at the end, just before his death, Berger's father had refused to talk about the heart condition that was slowly breaking him apart.

He stood up and turned to her, somehow managing to summon a smile. "We'll be okay, Sophie. You just concentrate on keeping the boys happy and I'll sort out everything else." The world seemed to shift around him, as if tightening its grip, and he stepped back and headed for the door. "I have a job to go to – one of the few on our books. We can talk more about this later."

Sophie nodded, hugging herself despite the spring morning being warm and bright. Standing there in the slanting daylight, she looked miles away, part of another world.

Berger drove north towards Otley, taking the back roads as much as he could. The rush hour was over but traffic was still heavy on the motorway. He was due at a house located near the airport to fix a faulty alarm system. Apparently the alarm went off at odd times of the day and night, triggered by nothing the owner could fathom.

He found the house easily. It stood, aloof and imposing, on a patch of ground at the end of a narrow street, a gap of about twenty feet between it and its closest neighbour. There was a council estate at the back of the property, and a shabby primary school around the corner.

Berger got out of the car and retrieved his tool box from the boot, then locked the doors before heading towards the house. The garden was neat and tidy; plants stood proud in the borders and the lawn was short. He walked up the concrete drive, noting the BMW parked with its nose against the garage doors, and knocked on the door.

There was a slight pause, and then the door was pulled open. A small man with narrow shoulders stood blinking into the day. "Yes? What is it?"

"Hello, sir. I'm Patrick – from Berger Alarms. You called me about your problem."

The man scratched his head; his hair was already dishevelled and the motion seemed to neaten it. "Ah, yes. Of course. You'd better come in, then."

Berger followed the man along a hallway hung with photographs – family portraits, houses, landscapes – and into a bright kitchen at the back of the property.

"I'm sorry if I seem flustered, but I had a late night last night. The bloody thing went off again. I'm sure the neighbours must hate me by now." Despite his complaints, the little man was smiling. "Cup of tea?"

"That would be lovely, Mr…Mr Eastman."

"Oh, call me Charlie," said the man as he turned to a counter and flicked the button on an electric kettle.

Berger located the wall-mounted plastic box containing the workings of the security system in a small alcove near the kitchen door. The problem was a simple one to resolve:

just a frayed wire and a loose connection. It took him only ten minutes to fix.

"That's marvellous, son. Thank you." Eastman handed Berger a cup, still smiling.

"I feel guilty for charging you a call-out fee for this, sir, but I'm afraid it's company policy." He sipped the tea; it was a herbal blend, and rather satisfying.

"No worries. In times like these, I expect prompt payment is what keeps small businesses afloat. At least that was certainly the case in my day." The man went to a shelf and took down a chequebook, then scribbled the appropriate sum and signed the bottom. He tore it from the book and handed it to Berger.

"Thanks. So, you've experience in running a small business?" Berger wasn't really interested, but the old man was pleasant enough company and the tea was rather delicious.

"Yes, I ran a small accounting firm for a few years after being made redundant from my job. It was a struggle, but turned out to be the best thing I ever did. No boss; no set working hours; all the profit was my own. I miss it now, and still keep my hand in, but I'm too old to work full time."

Berger tried to guess the man's age. Sixty-five? Seventy? The truth was, he barely looked a day over sixty, but if he was in fact retired he must be older. Certainly he was old enough that the current recession would barely leave a mark on him.

"I have my hobbies to keep me busy these days," said Eastman, glancing out of the kitchen window. "I enjoy a spot of gardening, do a lot of reading about the economy, and have a slight interest in the paranormal. Quite often these last two subjects make unlikely bedfellows."

Berger grinned. "Really? Ghosts and stuff? That's interesting. My wife likes to read about all that, but I'm afraid I'm a bit of a sceptic." The grin froze when he recalled his uneasy episode only that morning: the trick of reflection that had made him think a woman was standing in his garden.

Eastman shook his head. "So was I, Mr Berger, until I saw something. Just after my wife died, I witnessed her likeness walking across the back garden. She turned and looked at me for an instant, and then vanished into the shadows. Since then I've studied the subject quite extensively, and also how it relates to socio-economic factors."

Berger put down his cup. "You've lost me now. I'm just a simple electrician." He smiled, glanced at the door.

"Oh, it's nothing too complicated, just more examples of the so-called supernatural are reported during times of economic downturn. Some would say it's an example of people clinging to the hope of some kind of spiritual meaning during bad times, but I'd suggest periods of social turmoil and recession produce their own ghosts: actual spirits of the times."

"I see." Berger didn't see at all. If he was honest, he thought the old man might be just a little bit crazy. Perhaps the loss of his wife had affected him badly, or living alone in such a big house had twisted his mind towards strange matters. "Anyway," he said, changing the subject, "you should have no trouble with that alarm now, and if you do I'll come back and discount you the call-out fee."

Eastman nodded, smiled. "Thank you, Mr Bergman. And please, don't mind me and my idle talk. I have too much time on my hands and tend to come up with some odd theories."

The man accompanied Berger to the front door, and as he walked back down the drive, past the big car, he turned around to watch the door close. He thought of his own current troubles with his mortgage repayments and business being so bad, and wondered if perhaps Eastman had a point. If his theory even approached the truth, then Berger thought the spectres people saw in troubled times were more likely the result of stress than something supernatural.

He called into the office to find a heap of unpaid bills on his desk. Vanessa, the secretary, had been trying for days to call in money owed on outstanding invoices, but had experienced little success. They were owed a lot but their debts amounted to even more. It was becoming increasingly evident that Berger was going to have to make one of his small staff redundant. But who would it be? Tony Chong had been with him for years, and was a good worker – if a little sour of demeanour. Young Trev the apprentice was bright and cheery, eager to learn, and his meagre salary didn't make much difference to the company balance, anyway. Vanessa was the only person in the office dealing with admin, bills and accounts: she would be the last to go.

Considering the current light workload, it made sense that Tony be the one sacrificed.

Berger sat at his desk with his head in his hands, unable to even consider letting his workmate and friend go. He simply couldn't do it to the man. Yet…if he did nothing, the whole business might fail and they'd all be out of a job.

He looked at the little model windmill on his desk – the

pretty little folly Sophie had bought him one weekend in Whitby. It was a hand-made item, crafted with love and care, and seemed now to symbolise something greater than his problems. He pushed the tiny wood-and-leather sails of the windmill with his forefinger, watching them reluctantly move. If that motion was the economy, then it was stalled; no wind blew the windmill's sails, no produce was being processed within. The whole thing had ground to a halt.

The phone rang, drawing him out of himself, and he picked it up after a slight pause to refocus his thoughts. "Hello, Berger Alarms."

A voice was trying to be heard through the static, but Berger could not make out what it was saying.

"Can you speak up...or better still, ring me back? There's something wrong with the connection."

The line went dead.

Berger spent the rest of the day going through paperwork and ringing around suppliers. He managed to bring in some money the firm was owed, but it was not enough to make a difference. He told Vanessa he'd be back in the morning, and then returned home.

The twins were asleep upstairs so it was the perfect opportunity for a chat with Sophie.

"Things are bad, aren't they? I mean, *really* bad." Her eyes were dull; her skin looked old, wrinkled.

"I can't lie to you. Yes, we're in a bad way. I think I'm going to have to lay off Tony."

Sophie lowered her head. Her hands writhed in her lap like pained animals. It took him a while to realise she was weeping silently. "The twins are so expensive. I try to make the money stretch, I really do, but I have to buy two of *everything*."

"It's okay, honey." He went to her and put his arms around her thin frame, feeling how cold she was. Her face, when she looked up at him, was like a mask, a crude representation of what she might look like in another decade. "You look ill. Maybe you should go to bed."

She dried her tears and slumped against him. "I've been ill for weeks but I didn't want to add to your worries. My joints ache, my head hurts, I feel weak as a kitten. The doctor says its depression, but I can't allow that to happen."

Berger did not know what to do. "You need to be well, Sophie. The twins need you better. Just go to bed and rest for a while, and we'll make another appointment with the doctor. I'm sorry I didn't realise how badly you were suffering…it's been shit lately, and I've neglected you all."

She reached for him, her small hands flapping at his face. "No, you haven't. You've been trying to keep the business afloat."

"Some things," he said, truly believing it for the first time, "are more important than money." He looked around at their home, at the things held within it, and all of it seemed so pointless. What really mattered here were *people*, and somehow everyone had forgotten that simple fact on the way to realising their dreams of decadence.

That night Berger went for a drive. He'd been doing it for almost two weeks now, just driving through the streets and perhaps out into the country. It helped clear his mind, gave him some time and space away from his worries.

He guided the car through residential areas and past industrial centres, along narrow alleys and one-way streets. On the outskirts of Leeds, under a stone railway arch where shadows gathered like a crowd of beggars, he saw a figure detach itself from the abutment and glide across the road.

It was a woman, tall and willowy and dressed in what appeared to be a flowing black gown. Perhaps she was on her way home from a party or an event; maybe she was looking for a taxi rank. Berger stopped the car to let her pass, and tried to see her face. Darkness gathered around her features, obscuring them, and he could make out nothing but a strip of pale skin and dark, dark eyes.

It was only when the woman had gone that he remembered seeing her before. A week ago, out near the White Rose Centre, she'd been walking swiftly along the roadside verge with that same gliding motion. On that occasion too, he had been unable to make out what she looked like. Just white skin and black eyes; eyes so dark he'd assumed she was wearing too much eye shadow. It was certainly the same woman: he knew it as well as he knew his own name, yet he could not think why. Yes, her movements were the same, and even her appearance was identical to before, but this was a deeper truth than he could fathom.

Back at home, in the warmth and the darkness, he took off his coat and went upstairs. Bypassing the master bedroom, he continued along the landing and entered the twins' room. They were sleeping in the bunk beds, each curled onto the same side of their body and facing the wall. Bobby was sucking his thumb up above; Ben, on the lower bunk, held a small stuffed toy dog in his tiny fists, clinging to it as if it might save his life as he slept.

Berger knelt down by the bunks, kissed Ben on the temple, and then stroked Bobby's hot forehead until the boy murmured in his sleep.

"I'm failing you," he said, kneeling there before the heart of his existence, the meaning behind his struggle.

His face was wet. If the cost of giving his babies a good life, or at least of clinging to it for a little bit longer, was to make Tony Chong redundant, then the matter was out of his hands. These boys, his sleeping sons, came first, and that was all.

He went back downstairs and sat in the darkness. He stood and opened the living room curtains, staring out at the night. A figure ghosted out of the tall bushes at the end of the garden and stood watching the window. It was a woman, and she was clad in dark clothing; a flowing dress that reached her bare feet. Her hair was long, covering most of her face, but he could make out a large pair of smudge-dark eyes.

Berger opened his hand and pressed the palm against the window, smearing the glass. The woman took a small step forward, as if tentative yet unable to prevent herself from coming closer. Then she bowed her head and clasped her hands in an attitude of prayer.

The following morning was rough. Sophie looked tired and drawn, and the twins were boisterous. He ate breakfast with his fracturing family, hoping he could do enough to keep them together, and then kissed them all before leaving the kitchen. Sophie watched him go in silence. He grabbed the post on the way out the door, stuffing it into his pocket – a letter and two bills. The former was from the bank; he could tell from the envelope.

The drive to work was a nightmare: the heavy traffic seemed threatening, faces glared at him from behind windshields, and pedestrians seemed intent on walking in front of his car.

He pulled into his parking space and bent his head towards the wheel, feeling empty and hung-over despite not drinking the night before. The whole world was reshaping itself around the damage done by the bankers and financiers; the wounds torn so ruthlessly into the economy were scabbing over with a new and fragile tissue.

Shortly he got out of the car and went inside.

Then he waited for Tony Chong to arrive.

It did not take long; Tony was punctual in his habits.

"Can I have a word in the office?"

Tony nodded, took off his coat, and followed Berger into the inner sanctum.

"I think I know what's coming, mate. I'll spare you the agony of breaking it to me." Tony sat down, placed his hands on his knees, and swallowed. "I'll accept the redundancy package."

Berger was stunned. Had he been so stupid, so out of it lately, that he'd underestimated everyone around him? "I'm...I'm sorry, Tony. I've tried to keep things going the same for as long as I could, but something's got to give. I hate doing this to you."

Tony smiled, but it was a sad, worn-out expression threatening to slip at any minute. "I know you do. We're old friends, and if I can't understand this, then no one can. I'm the obvious one to cut. For Christ's sake, I've been twiddling my thumbs for almost a month now, waiting for work that was never going to come. I'm not daft. I know the score."

Berger felt like a shit because Tony was making this so easy for him. He would have preferred it if the man had stood and screamed, thrown the furniture, maybe even taken a swing at him.

"It goes without saying I'll be back in touch as soon as things get better." His words sounded hollow, bereft of weight and meaning.

"I know," said Tony, then he stood and left the room.

Berger took out the morning's mail. The envelopes were crumpled from being in his pocket. He selected the single letter: white paper, a small window in the envelope, the bank's return mailing address printed in cheap ink on the back.

He opened the letter.

As expected, it was a final demand before firm action was taken.

He did not want to lose the house, but now his hands were tied. He was powerless.

He sat there until Vanessa came in to say goodnight, then he sat for a long time afterward, just thinking about the mess they had made – all of them; the banks, the lenders, the people who'd bought into the capitalist dream.

"I can't do this," he said, looking up from his desk. A figure slipped out of sight, easing through the open door and out into the main office. He heard a whisper, like heavy material brushing against a desk or a wall, and then a breeze crept in, cooling his face.

Berger got up and followed her outside. He knew it was her; it could be no one else. The only question remaining was: who was she? *What was she?*

He trailed her across the car park – empty but for his vehicle – and onto the waste ground beyond. He kept his eyes locked onto her lissom form, drinking her in. There was a beauty to her that seemed...unearthly. Yet at the same time she was of the time, of the moment.

One of Charlie Eastman's spirits of the times…but no: that was just a mad idea concocted by a lonely old man. Because of Berger's financial troubles, he was allowing his mind to poke around in corners best left alone.

The concrete and asphalt became scrubland became dense loamy earth became thick, untrammelled grass. When Berger looked around, his gaze taking in the nature of the landscape, he saw open fields stretching into the distance. But right at the edge of his vision, just past the point where things began to blur and fade, he saw the distant flicker of flames. Fire was all around, in a vast and endless circle.

The sky was dark but it was deep; he sensed an ocean of possibilities above him.

The woman headed up a slight rise which turned into a hill without changing perspective. On top of the hill, its sails motionless, was the black silhouette of a windmill. The woman was heading towards the stubby structure, her pace increasing as she climbed.

Berger's breath was ragged; his legs ached. He realised with shame that his body was unaccustomed to such vigorous exercise and the muscles were rebelling.

It took a long time to mount such a small rise, but once at its crest he stopped and stared. Even close up, the windmill remained in silhouette: its walls and single window held no fine details. There was no door in its circular central tower. It was a crude rendering of a structure, a sketch, the idea or concept of a working building only partially realised. Form without function, shelter without purpose.

"What do you want? Why have you called me here?"

The woman said nothing. She simply stood with her

back against the blackened shape, her dress blowing in a wind Berger could not feel, her thin body swaying. He knew implicitly that he was meant to go to her: she had come as far as she could towards him, and now it was his turn to confront the thing he feared and could not understand.

He stepped forward.

The windmill's ragged sails slowly began to turn, as if nudged by a giant unseen hand. The sound of its gears was like the screams of the ruined, the cries of the unemployed and the unemployable, the wail of redundant tears. The flapping of the material wrapped around the framework of each sail was the fluttering of wings stunted before they were even allowed to fly.

"I need a way out of this. All of it. This isn't what I wanted when I was a child. It's not what I was promised in school and college and during my early days on the job. We bought the dream and the dream went sour."

The woman nodded her head once. Her hair did not move. Then, slowly, she stepped forward out of the shadows, at last able to come to him. As the sails turned and hazy moonlight made faint daggers across the ground at her small toeless feet, she finally emerged into view. Beneath the masking wash of dark hair, she had no mouth, and her nose was nothing but a small, neat hole at the centre of her face. But it was her eyes that Berger could not fail to notice, and to him they symbolised everything. If the eyes were indeed the windows of the soul, then the soul behind these ones was terrible.

In the shadow of her gaze, Berger knew this woman did not offer salvation.

Berger sank to his knees as the woman approached him,

her arm going up and out and the hand opening…and then falling onto his shoulder.

Then she looked down at him with those ugly black-slash eyes that were nothing more than barcodes, just like the ones stamped onto every consumable object available in stores and supermarkets all over the world, marked on each commodity mankind could stick a price on. She did not blink; the codes were incapable of movement. She just stared, logged his ultimate value and calculated the currency of his aspirations.

The frail ghosts of pounds and dollars and yen fell around him in a sudden storm of fiscal waste, and finally, and without further negotiation, she deemed his soul unworthy of discount…

#

Berger awoke much later, in his own bed, lying beside his wife. He knew it had not been a dream, but last night's experience had already begun to take on a dream-like quality.

He leaned across the bed and kissed Sophie on the cheek, being careful not to disturb her rest. Then he went into the twins' room and watched them for a while, filled with a sense of awe and wonder at the sight of their simple, uncomplicated beauty.

Downstairs, at the dining table, he took some notes from his wallet. Using an old cigarette lighter from the kitchen drawer, he burned the money on a saucer, watching fixated as the paper flared and then turned to ash.

Afterwards, when he stood and looked out of the window, admiring the first smudged colours of dawn on the horizon, he saw a thin dark-eyed figure standing by the fence, nodding in his direction. She would always be there, pulling the strings of society, but for once he could choose not to be her slave. There had to be another way – if not a better way, then simply an alternative to the one he had been born into. Whatever it was, he swore he would find it, and teach his children better lessons than the ones taught to him.

When dawn finally broke, bringing light into the world, Berger was surprised to find he was smiling.

The Row

The row of houses put me in mind of those sets from old Hollywood western films, the ones with a painted façade representing the buildings in a small town. Frames of timber and painted cardboard, all lined up along a dusty main street, with nothing behind the closed doors but cables, debris, and possibly an expanse of desert wasteland.

The street was like that. It had the feel of falseness, an ambiance of flimsy one-dimensional fakery being passed off as solid, three-dimensional reality.

The row of houses was located in east Leeds, in an area known for crime and poverty. Most of the neighbouring streets had been demolished – council houses well past their due date, torn down rather than being left to fall. This row, the only surviving part of what was once known as Sebastian Street, was all that remained: a fragile-looking line of eight houses, each one derelict. Wooden boards nailed across the window openings, steel security shutters in place of doors. It was a dead street, a kind of liminal space into which even the toughest street kids did not venture – not because they were afraid, but because they didn't even realise it was there.

Some places don't need ghosts to be haunted. Some places seem to haunt themselves from the inside out.

"I'll pick you up at about five-thirty. Is that okay?" Dan

sat in the driver's seat with his elbow poking through the open window, his arm resting on the frame. He stared dead ahead, watching the empty street.

"Yes," I said, scribbling down the time on the first sheet of paper attached to my clipboard. "That's fine. I have a packed lunch, and if I get desperate there's a pub a few streets away."

Dan turned to face me, his left eyebrow raised. "You'd have to be pretty damned desperate to go in The Feathers, mate. Roughest pub in the area, that is. I wouldn't send my worst enemy in there for a pint."

I nodded. "Okay, point taken. I'll stick with my sandwiches."

Dan smiled. "You'll be fine. None of the local crims or gangs goes near this place – there's nothing left here to steal; all the houses have been cleared out. Just be waiting for me when I come to pick you up, because I don't fancy hanging around." He winked, put the council van into gear, and pulled away from the kerb without saying another word.

I stood on the cracked footpath trying to compose myself. The street was strange, almost existing within a bubble of silence separating it from the usual urban clamour of vehicles, police and ambulance sirens, barking dogs and loud music drifting through open windows. The place had a strange sense of calm…no, that wasn't it, not exactly. It was more like a sense of isolation, as if it were cut off from the rest of the world.

I recalled what I'd read of the recent history of the row of houses during the desktop study I'd carried out back at the office. There had been only a handful of incidents worth reporting. In 1982 a woman's mutilated corpse was found inside one of the houses. Inside her naked and abused body were found traces of six different types of semen, including one from a horse, and a yard of bubble wrap. Her skin had been slashed by thin blades, probably scalpels. The killer – if indeed there was only one – was never found.

Glancing up and down the street, I checked my site plan against the reality before my eyes. Once this had been a long street, with terraced houses on either side, but now all that remained amid the bombsite wreckage of demolition was eight houses, their walls crooked, the brickwork scarred and dirty, the roofs bowed and showing patches where the tiles had been blown off in high winds. Nobody knew why these buildings had been left behind, but now it was finally time to tear them down and re-use the land for a new residential development. Like old bones, the building material would be carried away, ground to dust and used as landfill.

A wind whipped up, travelling along the street from west to east, stirring up the litter and rubble in the shattered gutters. Somewhere, a board groaned. As I looked up, feeling sad and alone, I watched a distant aeroplane draw a white line through the high blue sky. The place seemed to summon or invoke a sense of dread.

Shrugging off these dismal feelings, I made my way towards the first house. None of them had official house numbers, so in my notes I had simply numbered them as one to eight. It was good enough for my purposes.

The security shutters were padlocked, and I had the keys. Each one bore a paper tag corresponding to the numbers in my notes. I selected key number one and unlocked the shutter, then opened it to allow me access to the front door. The door was old, the paint was peeling off like damaged skin, and the timber beneath looked pale, like dried-out tissue. I pushed open the door – this one was unlocked – and a cloud of dust emerged to greet me. I stepped back, waving a hand in front of my face to ward off the musty odour of neglect, and waited for the dimness beyond the doorway to resolve into a room.

Back in the mid 1990s heroin addicts had used the row as a shooting gallery. Then, suddenly, they'd stopped coming here, as if something had happened to scare them away. The place had not been used by junkies since. Not even the occasional homeless person came here to sleep.

Despite the weak sun, the street seemed grey and unwelcoming. How much of this was simply down to a psychological reaction on my part, I cannot say. But the inside of the house was even darker, as if there were a barrier keeping out the daylight. Again, I suspect my mind was at least partially creating these effects, but nevertheless they were real enough at the time.

I adjusted my hard hat, tightened my grip on my bag, and walked forward, entering the house. For a moment it felt as if I were being enveloped in a giant fist. I was being pulled over the threshold rather than simply taking a few steps, but the sensation lasted only a moment – barely even long enough to register. It was only afterwards, when I began to examine my time there at the row of houses, that I fully appreciated what I had felt.

The door led straight into what was once a small living room. The ceiling and most of the first floor were long gone; when I looked up, I could see through the rotten joists right up to the roof. Dust hung in the air. The doorway leading to the kitchen was closed. I stepped gently across the uneven floor, trying not to trip on the piles of rubble, and opened the door. The kitchen was a mess, and when I walked in and looked to my right, I saw most of the dividing wall had been torn down to reveal the kitchen of the house next door. Standing there, in that position, it looked as if this process had been repeated along the entire row, as if some raging berserker had travelled the length of the row and torn down the walls, rampaging through each house.

I took a few snaps with my digital camera and then approached the ruined wall. Prodding around the area with a piece of timber, I decided the structure was not unsound. I took a few measurements, made a few notes, and stepped through into the next kitchen. The rooms were like the images on a photographic copy sheet: near identical scenes, the only differences being in the geometric patterns caused by the rubble. It felt like one long house, each room simply a continuation of the uninhabitable space before. That was the only sensation I experienced. I did not feel the presence of ghosts, or memories stirring in the dust. The row of houses was not haunted by restless spirits, but it did seem possible to me the derelict row might be haunted by the idea of what it had been before. Its past life as a street filled with life, with families living and eating and dying within its walls, haunted the place just as surely as any creaky old phantom.

I encountered nothing else strange or unusual that day, and when Dan returned to pick me up in the little council van, I was waiting for him at the kerb, facing the road and with my back turned on the row of houses soon to be demolished.

Dan dropped me off at home. He seemed distracted

during the journey, so we didn't talk much. He asked how things had gone during the survey, and I told him the structure was stable and I could start planning out a schedule of demolition works the following day. He nodded, kept his eyes on the road, and did not say goodbye when I got out of the van at my house.

Debbie was making dinner when I entered the kitchen. I'd walked in quietly, and she had the radio on, so she didn't realise I'd come in. I stood in the doorway and watched her, taking in her low-key beauty. She stuck out her lower lip and blew hair out of her eyes, stirring a pot of pasta sauce and moving her hips in time with the music.

She turned unexpectedly, probably registering at some deep level I was there and she was being watched, and when she did so the smile lit up her face as if someone were holding a flashlight under her chin.

"Evening." I walked further into the room, pulling out a chair and sitting down at the table.

"Good day?" She turned back to the stove, still stirring the pot.

"Not bad. Do you know that weird old row of houses on Sebastian Street?"

She nodded. "The creepy ones, nobody's lived there for ten years?"

"Yep. I did a survey. They're coming down in the next few weeks, and some new flats are going up in their place."

"Good," she said, turning off the heat. "That street is an eyesore. It should've been sorted out years ago." She drained the pasta, and then poured on the sauce.

I got up, went to the fridge, and took out a bottle of wine. I spotted a glass on the work bench, next to where

Debbie was cooking. "Top up?"

She glanced over, nodded. "You bet."

That night, as I lay in bed with a book, watching my wife undress, I experienced the uncomfortable feeling that something outside was examining us through the window. This made no sense, because the curtains were closed, yet still I felt scrutinised. I knew it wasn't a person, but perhaps some kind of consciousness was trying to understand us, the way we lived, the actions we carried out inside the rooms of our home.

When I slept, I dreamed of that row of houses on Sebastian Street, the security shutters removed from the doorways and the doorways themselves simply rectangles of blackness. Nothing moved in the darkness inside the houses, but I had the sense of frantic activity, of something scurrying between the buildings, using that manmade passageway between the kitchens.

I woke up sweating, with a scream lodged like trapped food at the back of my throat. Then I realised it wasn't a scream at all, and I vomited all over the bed sheets.

Debbie reached for me. "Are you okay?" She got out of bed and rushed around to my side, wiping my forehead with the palm of her hand. "God, you're hot. Like a radiator."

"I'm fine," I said, looking up at her, into her worried blue eyes. "Just a bug, or something."

Debbie stripped the bed and put the sheets in the washing machine as I cleaned myself up in the bathroom. It was too early in the morning to go back to sleep, so we went downstairs and drank hot, sweet tea until the sun came up. Debbie held my hand. I stared at the side of her face as she watched the daylight flaring beyond the kitchen window, her skin turning golden in the emerging rays.

The following week the row of houses was pulled down. The work went well; there were no problems encountered on site. The whole area was fenced off because of the exposed foundations, which would have to be broken up and removed before construction commenced on the new project.

I stood with Dan on the other side of the now flattened street, staring at the rubble. Diggers and muck shifters were parked on the site, workmen sat eating their packed lunches, and Dan smoked a hand-rolled cigarette.

"It actually improves this dump, don't it?" Dan smiled through a haze of smoke.

"I see your point," I said, taking a side step to escape the stench of cheap tobacco. "But doesn't it feel odd...empty? Like a vacuum?"

"Nah," said Dan, flicking his cigarette end onto the road. "It feels like a load taken off, a burden dropped. I always hated this street – those houses. If anywhere was going to be haunted, it would be them." He turned away and started talking to the foreman, and both men began to laugh.

I stared at the place where the row of houses had once stood, and imagined I could still see their outlines, shimmering in the dirty air.

In 2001 a child had gone into one of the houses – which one was never specified in the news reports – and not come out again. His friends witnessed the boy climbing in through a window where one of the boards had come loose, and then they waited for him for over an hour. When he failed to materialise, they went off and told their parents, who then called the police. The boy was never seen again. They did not even find a corpse.

Leaving the other men to their chatter, I walked across the road and strolled along the site boundary, gazing at the ground. I wasn't sure what I expected to find there, among the remains of the houses, but I do know I was disappointed when I did not discover anything. Not a bone, a fragment of human skull, or even weird effigies scrawled on the foundations. There was nothing – just broken bricks, shattered timber, the usual debris associated with an urban demolition site.

We went home early that evening. The work was done; everything was made safe. There was nothing left to do but post a security guard and wait for the construction squad to move in and commence their ground works.

I took a long bath when I got home, but when I emerged I still felt unclean, as if a filthy miasma clung to my skin and I could not get rid of it, no matter how hard I scrubbed. I had no idea why I felt this way, but I didn't mention it to Debbie.

We made love later that evening, but nothing seemed right. The rhythm was all wrong, and I felt ashamed of the imaginary dirt on my skin. As we moved awkwardly on the mattress, it felt as if we were being watched. I kept glancing over my shoulder, at the window, and expecting to see shadows shifting beyond the curtains.

"What's wrong," said Debbie, afterwards.

"I don't know. I think I'm just stressed. Maybe we need a holiday."

She gripped my hand under the sheets, and I squeezed her fingers.

"Yes," she said. "Perhaps that's it. A holiday. We haven't had one for a couple of years – not a proper one, anyway. I'll start looking tomorrow; see if there are any cheap deals going."

I said nothing. What I really wanted – what I needed more than anything – was a holiday from myself. If I could have stepped out of my skin, removing it like a costume, I would have traded it in for another, cleaner outfit. The filth of the row of houses on Sebastian Street – the *former* row of houses – was upon me, like a sticky ghost, and I could feel it working its way inside, penetrating my body through my pores to do untold damage within the walls of my frail house of bones and blood and organs…

I dreamt again of the row of houses. The doors were the black openings to coffins filled with endless night, and long, pale hands beckoned from within, calling to me, summoning me inside. I walked along the row, keeping to the middle of the road, and watched those white fingers dancing, trying to hypnotise me.

The dead lived in those houses, but I did not know their names. To me, they were just an abstract notion, an unspecified group of the damned who represented the concept of nothingness rather than anything tangible. These were the spirits of the houses, a bunch of lazy *genius loci*, and because I had been the last person to walk the floors of the places which housed them, I was cursed to see them here, in my dreams, perhaps forever.

I got out of bed, crossed the room, and opened the bedroom curtains. Outside, rather than the street I'd known for years, was a demolition site. Across the way, directly opposite my house, stood the row of derelict houses from Sebastian Street, misplaced and somehow planted here, right where I lived. The doors were open, belching blackness, and as the shadows moved slowly across the road, towards my front door, I saw held within them the shapes of all the people who had dwelled in the row and those who had never got the chance to live there. The dreams to which the houses themselves had once aspired left to rot, to turn into something dark and malign and grasping.

Because houses dream, too, and sometimes those dreams are nightmares.

Debbie was not in bed beside me when I woke from the dream, hot and clammy and filled with a shapeless fear that punched me from the inside, trying to get out. I rolled out of bed and ran onto the landing. "Debbie!" I could smell fresh coffee, but she did not answer. "Debbie? Are you down there?" I ran down the stairs, almost tripping at the bottom, and into the kitchen.

The kitchen was empty. The coffee machine light was on; two empty cups sat on the bench.

Panicked, I searched every room in the house, calling her name, but she wasn't there. She was nowhere to be seen.

Then, defeated, I sat down in the living room and stared at the silent television, imagining her trapped inside those dream houses, chased by something large and unseen through the passageway between the kitchens.

Then I heard the front door open and slam shut.

I ran out into the hallway, and saw Debbie struggling with a shopping bag.

"Give me a hand, would you?"

I moved quickly, taking the bag as she stumbled through the doorway. "Where have you been?"

"We were out of milk, so I decided to do some shopping. We needed quite a bit." She stared at me, her eyes narrowing. "Why, what's wrong?"

"I had another nightmare."

She looked at me like a teacher reassuring a small child. "Oh, you poor boy."

"Stop it," I said. "I dreamt something had happened to you – I know that sounds lame, but for a minute there, I believed it. I...I panicked when you weren't here."

"I'm sorry." She moved towards me, closing the door. "I didn't mean to tease you. It's just...well; you don't usually act like this."

I shook my head. "You mean weak? I'm not usually this weak?"

"Come on, let's have breakfast. All I meant is you never have nightmares. Not in all the time I've known you have you had a nightmare. Maybe you really are stressed."

She was right. Even as a child, I'd never experienced bad dreams. I'd just never had them...until now. I was infected, as if the nightmares of those sleeping houses had somehow seeped into me, burrowing into my brain to metastasise like a cancer. I was under their influence. The demolition had let out their dreams and they had come into me...

I did not go in to work that day. My boss reacted kindly when I told him I had a virus, and I hadn't slept at all the previous night. He told me to rest, to come back only when I felt better. The work would still be there when I returned. I did not enjoy lying to him, but nor could I face going into the office, or, worse still, going out to inspect another building site.

Debbie looked after me; she made sure I had plenty to read and a constant supply of DVDs. The day passed slowly, and I started to feel better. I even began to doubt my previous ill feelings about the row of houses on Sebastian Street, and wondered what was causing me so much stress I would imagine such things as communicable nightmares and the ghosts of dreaming houses…

"Feeling better?" Debbie handed me a mug of tea. "You look better. The colour's come back into your cheeks." She sat down beside me and took my hand. I wanted to apologise, to say sorry for being such a weak man.

"Yes, thanks." I sipped my tea. It was too hot so I put it down on the coffee table.

"I was online earlier and found a cheap holiday. Greece. In a little villa by the sea. I thought we could book it this evening. It would give us something to look forward to." She smiled, kissed my cheek, rubbed my chest.

"That's great," I said. "I think you're right. We should book it. Let's not wait."

"Okay, I just need to tidy up a bit first, and then I'll sort it out. I think this'll be good for us." She touched my shoulder, lightly. "Good for you. I'm not sure what's gotten in to you lately, but you've been acting strange."

I sighed. "I know. I'm sorry. I haven't a clue what's going on inside my head, but I sometimes feel like I'm losing my grip."

Debbie's fingers ran along the line of my throat, tickling me. "We'll be fine. This holiday will make everything good again. I know it will. A little trip away always makes people feel better." Her smile was brief, but it was warm and filled with love.

She went upstairs to the study, her steps quick and light on the carpet. Somehow her footsteps seemed to rise much too high in the house, towards levels that did not exist, as if she were moving too far away from me and I might never get her back. I thought again of that ghostly row of houses on Sebastian Street, and how my first impression of them had been of a façade, a false front built to conceal something no human eye had ever seen. What if relationships are like that? The walls we build to keep the darkness at bay. And what happens when those walls are breached?

"Debbie…"

It was like an emotional echo of what I had felt earlier, when I'd thought Debbie had vanished. But this time it was for real; this time she really was leaving me, and if I didn't do something I might never see her again.

She kept climbing. I could hear her footsteps above my head, moving in all directions: left, right, up, down, and up again. She was ascending an imaginary staircase, one that had never existed and could not exist in the real world. But maybe it existed in that liminal space behind the façade, the one the row of houses on Sebastian Street had always concealed…until someone had come along and pulled them down.

Why had they never been demolished with the rest of the street? What purpose could they have served, standing there like sentinels? I remembered reading somewhere that even when the other houses on the street had been inhabited, those eight had remained without tenants, and nobody had even enquired about buying or renting them.

Sentinels…guarding us all against the onslaught of something…something terrible, something nightmarish which had always wanted to straddle the façade and enter this side of the screen, occasionally reaching through to pollute the world it so coveted.

I recalled the dead woman found there with her body

slashed and torn and plastic packaging rammed up inside her, the terrified junkies who'd run away and never returned; and finally, I thought of the small boy who had entered one of the properties and never come back out again…was he even now endlessly walking through the empty rooms, looking for an exit and wondering if his friends were still waiting outside for him?

Debbie's footsteps kept on moving, rising, through levels I could never see. I got to my feet and ran to the bottom of the stairs, looked up and watched as the staircase bent and twisted, whipping to and fro like a snake with its tail stuck in a vice. I blinked, trying to erase the vision, but it was real: the staircase was moving, shuddering, spiralling madly, like part of a fairground funhouse.

"Debbie!"

I ran to the crazy moving staircase and started to climb, but the violent bucking movement threw me off. I tried again, and the banister turned to dust beneath my fingers. I fell to the floor, into a pile of rubble, and when I looked up the stairway had stopped moving, it was motionless. But it wasn't the staircase that had always been in my house…it was from somewhere else.

When I looked around me, at the bare walls and the snapped floorboards, the piles and heaps of debris, I realised exactly where I was: I was inside one of the houses on Sebastian Street. There could be no mistake; the image of the place nestled deep inside me, and now that it had come back to haunt me I knew it intimately.

The stairway above me terminated in fresh air; the upper landing had fallen away, leaving only empty space. Joists and the skinned, tattered ends of boards protruded like broken teeth. There was no point in even trying to go up there. Debbie was somewhere else entirely.

I heard something moving behind me, as if stepping through rubble, and when I turned around I saw the kitchen doorway. I got up and walked towards it, entered the wrecked kitchen, turning right to face the place where the wall had been torn down to gain access to the building next door. I saw a vague human form disappearing into darkness a few rooms along, a small running figure swallowed by dusty shadows.

"Debbie!" My voice did not echo. The word fell flat and dead upon the floor.

I stepped through the gap and into the kitchen of the house next door, following the slender figure of my wife as she moved between the houses. The row had taken her, snatched her away from me, and all I had left was the urgency of pursuit. I called her name again, but this time the sound barely even registered in the chill, dead space. Not even as a whisper.

#

Someday, if I shout loud enough, I hope my wife will hear me. One day, hopefully some time soon, I will catch up with her as I move back and forth through the passageway between houses, passing through the rooms between rooms, and it will give me hope – all the hope I will ever need.

Because houses dream, too, and sometimes those dreams become nightmares. Some places don't need ghosts to be haunted. I am the only ghost in this place, the lost spirit that walks between the walls. This unseen row of houses is inhabited at last, but only by the sound of my screams.

When One Door Closes

Another day, another failed interview…

Nick was beginning to suspect there was something wrong with him – some physical or mental imbalance he could not see but everyone else picked up on as soon as he walked into a room. That would explain how, no matter what he did to impress them, no one wanted to employ him. He had attended several job interviews over the past month, since losing his job at the packing factory, but nothing else had come up to fill the gap and replenish the coffers.

Maybe he had somehow become *unemployable* (an awful word; the one they spoke only in a whisper at the Job Centre). Was it like a permanent mark on his flesh, or a giveaway in his walk or the way he held himself? Was it so obvious he didn't really want the fucking jobs anyway? That he saw nine-to-five work only as a way of paying the bills while he waited for the world to notice his novel?

Nick walked down the high street with his hands stuffed in his pockets, fingers clutching his empty wallet and the scant few coins he'd managed to salvage to pay his bus fare. It was all becoming so depressing; all these job interviews amounting to nothing, not even a paltry second interview.

He ambled to the bus stop and joined the back of the queue. He stared at the back of the head of the man in front of him: greasy hair, flaky scalp. When the bus finally arrived the queue shuffled forward, as slow and orderly as a Russian bread line. The people climbed aboard one by one. When Nick reached the doors he was shocked to see them jerk shut, and to hear the bus hissing at him like a big, angry cat.

He looked through the grimy plexi-glass, at the fraught and overweight driver. The driver shrugged, fiddled with his control panel, and when the doors still refused to budge he shrugged again. The bus moved slowly away from the kerb, joining the traffic like a fish entering a migrating shoal in some busy gulf stream.

Feeling like this was some kind of metaphor for his day, Nick set off on the short walk home. At least this way he could save some money; the coins in his pocket might be put to better use elsewhere.

Annie was there when he got home, eating a sandwich and reading a newspaper at the kitchen table. "Hi," he said. "I didn't get it." He had learned some time ago to pre-empt her questions; this way the conversation did not go on for long and he was spared at least some of the shame he associated with constant rejection.

"Another dead end, eh?" Her eyes remained focused on the paper. "Jesus, you could use some luck." She frowned, but he could not be sure if it was over the news item or his report of yet another unsuccessful meeting.

Annie finished her lunch and put the plate in the sink, then leaned forward to distractedly kiss his cheek. Her lips were cold and damp. They left crumbs on his skin when she pulled away. "I have to rush off – only came back for lunch, to save some pennies." The smile didn't touch her eyes; they remained narrow and hard and unfocused.

"See you tonight." Why did that sound so much like a question?

Annie didn't reply. She just went out the back door and disappeared through the gate.

Nick shuffled over to the sink and filled a glass with water. There was a chip in the glass – a small imperfection – and he twisted it so the sharp edge faced away from him, so it wouldn't touch his mouth.

He wasn't hungry so he didn't bother with lunch. Instead he made instant coffee and read Annie's paper – the Guardian, the fucking *Guardian*? Who the hell was she trying to impress? She only ever used to read the tabloids, but since starting her new job at the financial company, her reading tastes had changed. It was as if she were trying to exclude him from that side of her life: the side where she held down a respectable job in an office full of Guardian readers...

About an hour later he decided to go upstairs and clean the bathroom. Might as well utilise his time productively, and God knew the job needed doing. If he didn't get into the habit of carrying out these little household chores, he knew he would grow increasingly idle. He wasn't even in the mood to write – he kept saying to Annie that he was "between novels" but the truth was he had invested everything in the one novel he had sent to a list of literary agents gleaned from the internet one slow, dull afternoon over a month ago.

Putting all his eggs in one basket... It was a line he'd cringe at if he read it in a book, and he certainly wouldn't use it in his own writing. But, like most clichés, the phrase served better than any he could concoct himself.

He put the coffee cup on the draining board and headed for the door, his mind caught up in dreams of literary stardom. Reaching out, he grasped the door handle and turned, but the door didn't open. It stayed jammed in its frame, not budging an inch. Puzzled, Nick twisted and turned, turned and twisted...but he could not open the door.

After countless minutes engaged in this increasingly futile endeavour, he began to sweat and his fingers ached as if he'd bruised them. He moved away from the door, rubbing his hands together, and sat down at the table. He stared at the door. The locked door: the locked door that didn't even *have* a lock. He felt bewildered and strangely hurt, as if this was yet another example of how the world was conspiring to shut him out. Or, as in this case, to shut him in.

Nick waited a few minutes and then tried the door again, but the same thing happened. The door, he reasoned, must have got stuck in the wooden frame. Something in the mechanism had broken and become lodged in the latch or something.

He went to the back door and pulled the handle. That too was locked. Agitated now, he took his key from his pocket and tried to unlock the back door. But nothing happened: the key just spun in the lock, as if it was meant for another lock altogether.

Fear nudged up close to him in the small kitchen, pressing its nose against his face. This was insane – things like this didn't happen, not in the real world and not to normal, everyday people. Once again he tried the doors; and once again they remained shut.

Nick sat down at the table and stared at his hands. Wide fingers, broad knuckles: the hands of a car mechanic, not an artist. Why the hell had he even thought someone would be interested enough to want to read his novel?

Later, Annie came home and walked blithely into the kitchen. The door leading out into the hall – the one Nick had been unable to open for hours – opened with ease.

"What's up? You don't look like you've moved since lunchtime?" There was humour in her voice, but with a hint of irritation at its edges.

"I…you're not going to believe this, but I've been stuck in here since you left."

Annie stood framed in the doorway. Her weight was balanced neatly on one hip, and she stared at him with a cool detachment. Her lips were curled up into a disbelieving little half smile. Her blonde hair shimmered beneath the bright overhead kitchen light. She looked smart and sassy, like a TV lawyer, in her Dorothy Perkins suit and shiny shoes. "Don't talk shite," she said, ruining the illusion.

"I've been having some trouble lately. With doors." Said aloud, it sounded stupid. Nick wished he'd kept it to himself.

Annie moved into the room, went to the sink and filled the kettle. "What are you on about? Trouble with Doors…isn't that the title of a book or a play, or something? Something by Pinter?" She stood facing the kettle, waiting for it to boil and no doubt enjoying her smart-arse comment. The old Annie – the one who read tabloid newspapers and celebrity magazines – would not even have known who Pinter was.

The heating element clicked and clacked; Annie didn't turn around.

"It started about a week ago. Doors sticking in their frames, and then closing in my face even when there was nobody on the other side." His voice was flat, but there was little he could do to lift it, to add any emotion. He barely believed in what he was saying, so why should she?

"Just stop being so stupid, Nick. I'm a little bit bored with your excuses these days. 'The post was already filled,' 'they already had someone lined up for the job,' 'my bus was late so I missed the interview.'" The kettle started to boil: the sound was like an asthmatic drawing frantic breaths. "You're living in a dream land. That novel isn't going to make you a millionaire. In this financial climate, you'll be lucky if anybody even picks it up off the slush pile."

Financial climate: another phrase he'd never heard her use before. Slush pile: that was another one.

Nick stared at her back, at her firm arse clad in the tight black skirt. He couldn't remember the last time they'd made love, but he did remember it had been a disaster.

"Just get a job. *Please*, get a job." Now she did turn to face him, and her eyes were red and sore-looking. She wiped a hand across her face, blinked, and breathed out. "You want coffee?"

He nodded, unable to think of anything to say.

Later that night he went upstairs to bed. Annie was lying on her front, her head buried in the pillows. During the early days of their relationship, this had worried him: he was often terrified she might suffocate in her sleep. He climbed into bed and reached out to her, stroking her bare arm. She moaned, shifted, and then went silent.

Nick stared up at the ceiling, still stroking Annie's arm. His gaze slid down the wall, and then across to the door. He couldn't be sure in the darkness, but it looked as if the door was slowly closing, the small gap between door and frame reducing to zero. Then, shockingly, it shut with an audible bang.

"I'm sorry." Annie's voice was tiny in the darkened

room. "I didn't mean to get at you earlier."

"I know." He kept stroking; maybe if he kept it up long enough she might realise how much he loved her.

"It's just so difficult. You seem to be sitting around and waiting for something to happen, while all the time life's passing you by…"

"I'll try harder." He closed his eyes. Stroked her arm. "I'll do better."

"I know you will." Her voice was fading; she was entering sleep. "I know…" Then she said nothing more.

The next day he left the house with Annie and walked with her to the bus stop. When the bus arrived they kissed stiffly and he watched her climb aboard. She didn't glance at him through the window, but he stood there watching anyway until the bus vanished from sight.

He walked into town, needing the exercise. Last night's slight altercation with Annie had served to focus his thoughts. He needed to do something positive, and today's interview might just be the kick-start he needed.

Entering town, he headed for the canal and started running potential questions and answers through his head: *Why should we give you this job?* Because I believe I can be an asset to this company. *What are your main assets other than your qualifications?* I'm loyal, a team-player, and strive for perfection in everything I do.

It was all utter bullshit of course, but he needed to tell them what he thought they wanted to hear. That was the art of a good interview: to give them what they wanted but without making them realise they wanted it.

He walked past new office buildings and multi-storey car parks whose external walls were mounted with CCTV cameras, feeling as if he'd entered some kind of Gerry

Anderson version of the future – a clunky vision, imagined decades ago, when none of the current technology existed. Everything seemed deliberately false, plastic, like a film set after the cast and crew have all gone home.

Annie's last job had been somewhere nearby, but now she worked out of town, where the office rental was cheaper and the rush-hour traffic wasn't as bad. Everyone else was struggling, but she had used the weak job market and skills shortages to her advantage and switched to a better firm. She was leaving him behind; passing through doors he couldn't even see let alone open.

Finally he reached what he thought was the correct building. He checked the address against the computer print-out given to him at the Job Centre, and once he was certain they matched he headed up the wide concrete steps and towards the main entrance.

He put out his hand and palmed the door, but it remained closed. Stopping in his tracks, Nick tried again, but the door failed to respond. He stared though the glass, at the security guard sitting behind the counter, and the man reached under his desk to buzz Nick inside. The buzzer sounded, but once again the door refused to open.

The guard hastily got to his feet and quick-stepped across the foyer, looking confused and embarrassed. He opened the door – easily, oh so easily – and stepped out of the way. "Sorry about that, sir. It must be playing up." His smile was troubled, as if he couldn't understand why the door had not opened in the first place.

Nick signed in and was directed by the same security guard to a company who occupied space on the second floor. He waited for the lift, and when the doors opened several people stepped out and to either side of him, like waters breaking around a rock. He slipped inside as the doors began to shut, and pressed the button for the second floor.

He was stuck in the lift for fifteen minutes, until finally someone else summoned it from the second floor and he was able to slip out through the opening doors.

Each time it had reached his floor prior to that moment the lift had simply continued on its way, climbing and falling through the levels until he had begun to lose his grip on the situation.

Breathing heavily, Nick stumbled out of the lift and made his way along the corridor. People came and went, appearing through doorways and passing him by in the corridor, giving him quizzical looks. He felt hemmed in; trapped in his own skin. The whole world looked like it was made up of closing doors.

The reception area beckoned: the door was open, inviting him to step inside. Nick moved towards it, his feet brushing on the tiled floor, and just as he was within touching distance of the door it slammed shut. The sound was deafening. There was no one in the immediate vicinity who could have slammed the door in his face. It had simply happened, like so much else in his life simply happened. Except nothing at all about this was simple…

Nick stood there, cut off from his possible future. He looked through the glass door like a kid with his face pressed up against a cake shop window, desperate to step inside and dig into the display.

He tried the door, knowing exactly what would happen…and inevitably, the door would not move. He turned around, looking for help, and a row of doors lined up along the corridor all slammed in unison, as if teasing him.

Nick felt like screaming, but he held it inside. If he let go, he feared he might not be able to put a stop to the madness churning in his stomach. He faced forward, towards the door, closed his eyes, and prayed...prayed to whoever or whatever might be listening...prayed to forces he did not understand or even believe in...prayed to whatever cruel god was toying with him...

Suddenly, the door wrenched in his hand; someone was tugging it open from the other side. He stepped back, pulled back his hand, and watched a large woman squeeze awkwardly through the gap. "Oh," she said. "Sorry." She smiled, moved aside, and Nick slipped through before the door closed, thanking her and just about keeping his emotions in check.

"I'm Nick Handy," he said to the woman behind the reception desk. "I have an interview." The woman smiled, but her features were flat and empty beneath the mask. She glanced up at him as she checked her list, and when finally she found his name the smile brightened, becoming more real.

Nick waited, eyeing the doors, all the doors leading off this single main room.

"I'm afraid you're a little late, Mr Handy, but you'll still be seen if you'll wait a while. There's a waiting room over there." She pointed with her pencil, and then looked away, dismissing him in an instant.

Nick lurched for the door – a man was holding it open, chatting to another person just inside the room. Then, abruptly, the person inside stood up and walked out of the door, starting to close it behind them.

Nick dodged past the departing man, smiling, and

slipping his leg through the narrowing gap. The door closed against his knee, trapping him momentarily, but he forced his way inside. The door clicked shut. The two men outside frowned at him, and then laughed softly before moving away.

The room was small, and there were far too many doors. Five or six, each one leading to another room where things Nick could not understand were being discussed; where strange plans and ideas were being pondered. Suddenly this interview was the last thing he wanted to sit through, but he knew he was trapped here, in the waiting room, at least until someone opened the door to let him out.

He sat down on one of the chairs and then stood up again. He was restless; his mind and body were wired, unable to calm down.

He felt strange and alone and...*locked out*. He felt locked out, even though he was effectively shut inside.

Nick stood at the centre of the room, turning in a slow circle and addressing each door in turn. "Why?" he said, quietly. "Why are you doing this to me?"

He pointed at each door, his hand shaking.

His fingers trembled. His blood thundered.

The doors were impassive; they were not alive or sentient, no matter what Nick might think. They were doors. Just doors.

"*Why?*"

At first nothing happened – there was no visible response. But then the lights in the room flickered for a moment before going out, leaving him in a murky gloom not nearly dark enough to be called true darkness; just a bland, grey space lacking any kind of natural daylight. He could see clearly the outlines of the furniture, the locations of the doors set into the walls.

Thoughts and images spooled through his head, flickering not unlike the failing light had done seconds before: all the interviewees who'd ever turned him down, Annie's face when she realised he wasn't coming home, the novel he'd written, the countless other novels he might have produced if he had only been given an iota of encouragement…if only the right doors had opened.

History, all of it: memories of a life now rapidly fading.

Then, simultaneously, the doors slowly opened, snickering like vertical mouths. Nick looked at the handles; then at the hinges; then at the rectangular panels which made up each individual door.

And finally he stared at the narrow black apertures between doors and frames: sly and shivering tooth-lined slits widening to allow whatever blackness lurked beyond to reach out and touch him.

The Chair

The long winter evenings were hardest of all: when daylight ended early and the darkness which took its place was hard and flat as sheet metal, Ben waited in vain for his father's shadow to arrive. He waited for so long and so often that it became habit, a ritual like so many others that made up his existence.

He sat forlornly at the living room window and watched the street, wishing his father's car would appear, slowing as it approached the house to turn into the empty drive. His mother was usually busying herself in the kitchen – plating up a sparse meal for tomorrow, preparing his medication, or mixing herself a cocktail – and Ben's shoulders tensed at every sound she made. The laboured twist of a lid. The eager chink of a glass. The deep sighs which bled from her willowy frame as she sat down heavily at the table to drink.

The street, however, remained empty and silent but for the occasional lone figure passing beneath the cold glare of streetlamps or a huddled group of strangers returning home from the pub. None of these passers-by made much noise; they simply went on their way, leaving the street and its inhabitants unmolested.

One night at the start of December, just as the temperature was beginning to drop sharply towards full winter, Ben sat at his usual place by the window, chin resting on his fists, knees tucked up under his body as he waited for something to happen.

"Would you like a drink?" His mother's voice slurred – it always was by this time of the day. Her evening cocktails had become more frequent; she was rarely seen without a glass in hand.

"No thanks." He continued to watch the street.

"A sandwich, maybe? Or a bowl of that cereal you like so much?"

Ben shook his head, aware his mother could not see his response but realising that one was not really needed. She did not offer him anything more.

They watched a gameshow where screaming contestants – each more overweight than the last – tried to guess the retail prices of electrical appliances, and then it was time for bed. Ben kissed her cheek, drawing back as soon as his lips made contact with her wet, rubbery skin, and then he headed for the door. He could not recall the last time his mother had tucked him in, although he knew she always entered his room before she retired to her own bed. She usually stood for a few minutes at the bottom of his bed, weeping, while Ben fought hard to convince her he was dreaming. He could not guess what her reaction might be if she knew he was awake.

"Don't forget to take your tablets." His mother spoke without taking her eyes from the television screen; they reflected a capering man in a grey suit, a drab audience perched on the edge of hysteria.

Ben took the small plastic cup from the mantelpiece and swallowed the three white pills dry, wondering what might happen if he ever forgot about them.

Upstairs, after brushing his teeth and emptying his bladder, Ben sat at his desk, staring at the sky beyond the streaky window. Big dark clouds shuffled across the vast grey expanse, seeming to rise and fall as they travelled across the horizon. Faces appeared within them, eyes and noses and gaping mouths...the disinterested gods of his empty childhood.

Standing, Ben leaned upwards to open the window and let in a sharp breeze – the air inside the room was thick and heavy, as if carrying elements of his sorrow. As he pushed the latch into its socket, jamming the window open an inch and feeling the cold air brush against his cheek, he glanced down and saw the chair. It was perched outside a house a few doors along the street, positioned in the footpath central to the gate of the property. It was an old dining chair: wooden back and legs, a beige plastic-coated cushion on its seat. The cushion looked worn, faded; its shape was lumpy.

Ben was puzzled. Why would someone place a dining chair out there, right in the front street? If it had been left out for disposal by the bin men, it was a few days early (bin day wasn't until Friday and today was only Tuesday). He supposed the sight of the solitary chair might not be so strange during the summer, when it was conceivable that someone might have left it out after spending an afternoon lounging in the sun. But it was winter, and it was cold – the coldest he could remember in his short life. The weather reports were all predicting heavy snowfall by the end of the week, and a few dusty white flakes had even begun to fall earlier that evening.

No, the chair was a mystery, an oddity: something to distract his thoughts. What made it even more peculiar was that Ben could not shake the feeling he had just missed seeing someone sitting in the chair; if he had been quicker he might have witnessed someone standing up and walking away. The idea was frightening, yet it also made him feel alive.

The chair was gone when he got out of bed next morning. He'd dreamed of it, imagining a tall, straight-backed figure sitting there all through the night, so it was fresh in his mind when he woke. He almost ran to the window and the sight of the empty spot on the footpath provoked a dull ache of disappointment in his stomach.

Ben turned away from the window and went downstairs, where he prepared his own breakfast. The plastic cup had been replaced on the mantelpiece – its rightful place, where both Ben and his mother would always see it – and three new pills sat at the bottom. He picked up the cup, poured the pills into his hand, and then walked back into the kitchen. He dropped the pills into the sink and turned on the cold tap. It took a long time for them to swirl down the plughole.

"Wow," he said, taken aback by his small act of rebellion. He tried to come up with a reason for not taking the pills, but none would come. He simply felt like missing a dose.

His mother emerged from her room as he was eating cereal. He heard her heavy footfalls above him, moving slowly across the landing. The bathroom door slammed shut. By the time his bowl was empty the toilet was being flushed. The sound was too loud, as if there was something wrong with the plumbing; pipes banged on the walls, like tiny fists demanding release from an unseen prison.

As his mother's footsteps creaked down the stairs, Ben choked back the urge to scream. Had the missed medication upset the delicate balance of his nerves? Surely, he thought, any side effects would take much longer to surface.

"Sleep okay?" His mother's eyes were barely open; her

face was slack, like an empty bag. She had neglected to comb her hair and her dressing gown was buttoned up all wrong. "Did you get your breakfast?"

"I always do," said Ben, but the words did not find their target.

Later that day it began to hail. The sky darkened and splits opened up within it, letting loose a mixture of rain and ice sounding like gunshots against the window panes. Ben sat on the sofa and watched in awe: he'd always loved these extremes of weather. Rain, snow, hail…these things excited him in a way that he failed to comprehend but enjoyed anyway.

His mother stayed in the kitchen a long time, sitting at the dining table and nursing a bottle. Ben entered the room several times that morning, but his mother never moved. She stared at the same spot on the wall for hours, her eyes like stones pushed into the damp unmoving mask of her face.

The telephone rang some time between noon and one o'clock. Ben stirred from his place at the window and picked up the receiver. The storm outside sounded loudly in his ear – too loud to properly make out the voice straining to be heard.

"Hello?"

"– couldn't do it. Not coming…going away–"

"Hello? Who is this?" The line was breaking up, swallowed by static. "Dad?"

The voice went quiet as soon as Ben said the word. The static cleared, yet whoever was trying to speak suddenly clammed up, as if reluctant to reveal himself. The moment stretched past its breaking point. Ben glanced at the clock on the wall, but could not seem to fathom the time.

"Is that you, Dad?"

The static swelled one final time, then broke apart, leaving behind a gap into which a voice stumbled: "I'm sorry, son. You have to believe that. I never wanted any of this to happen – it wasn't what I planned. Just remember I love you and I'll see you again…just not now. Not yet."

Was his father crying? Was that why the voice sounded so strained, so unlike the one he'd heard all his life, gently encouraging him from the background, urging him to be better, to face the things he feared? "Dad."

The line went dead. Ben replaced the receiver, surprised at how steady his hands were. Missing his medication that morning seemed like a blessing – usually, after such an awkward moment of social interaction, his hands would be twitching like frightened rabbits. He smiled, but the expression felt wrong on his face, like a wet rag pressed against his lips.

"Who-was-that?" His mother could barely construct a sentence: it came out as a single word.

"No one," said Ben, satisfied he was still able to lie to her, to make her believe he was doing okay and everything would turn out fine, in time, after the remains of battle had been tidied away.

They did not speak again for the remainder of that day.

The chair was outside again that night when he went upstairs.

Ben went to bed early just to check, and it sat in the same place outside the same gate, on the same part of the footpath. He once again had the sense that the chair had been recently occupied – very recently; as if, in fact, whoever had been sitting there had got up and left the exact moment before Ben looked in its direction.

On closer inspection he could see the chair's cushion was badly damaged. A split indentation marred its otherwise unbroken surface, as if a body too heavy had sat there for far too long. Ben tried to remember who lived there, in the house outside of which the chair had appeared, but could not recall any overweight resident. In fact, he was sure he'd never seen anyone coming or going from the property apart from a small old lady who only ever seemed to potter around in the garden, pruning the bushes and digging in the wide soil borders.

He pressed his forehead against the window pane, trying to get closer to the chair without actually leaving the house. He had not left the house for several months – he wasn't sure quite how many; certainly almost as long as his father's absence, which had occurred immediately after the final argument between his parents. To go outside now would take an act of will his medication was designed to smother.

Was that why he'd chosen to miss his pills? He'd done the same this evening, before climbing the stairs – holding them in the side of his cheek until he could reach the bathroom to flush them away. He'd watched as they swirled in the pan, little white pellets caught up in a storm.

Ben's eyes ached but he could not blink. He was afraid if he moved his gaze from the chair for even a split second, he might miss catching sight of its owner. For some reason, the thought of this filled him with a horror that felt bigger than the house, even larger than the sky above it: a gargantuan terror that could not be allowed into the open.

He sat at the window until his eyelids grew too heavy to support and his body began to slump. Tiredness dragged him towards his bed, and he was sleeping even before he fell lifelessly onto the soft mattress.

His mother failed to rise the following morning. All during breakfast he waited for the sounds of her stirring, but by 11 a.m. she still had not shifted. He imagined her dead up there, lying flat and stiff having choked on her tongue during the night; or perhaps she'd suffered a sudden heart attack in her sleep. He put it off for as long as he could, but by the time morning TV became afternoon TV he knew he must investigate.

Ben climbed the stairs with feet as heavy as his conscience. He crossed the landing and stood outside his mother's bedroom door, hands hanging limp by his sides, feet pointed slightly inwards. After what seemed like hours he finally reached out to open the door. His sweaty hand clenched the handle and he pushed open the door, flinching as its bottom edge scraped with a sound like claws across the too-thick carpet.

"Mum?"

There was no answer. The room was dark and silent. Not even a chink of light could be seen through the closed curtains. His mother hated the daylight; she was a light sleeper, and even the slightest hint of illumination in the room would wake her. She'd bought special blackout curtains to hang at the windows, and the darkness they produced was thick as tar and just as hard to penetrate.

"Mother?" That was better: the more formal address felt comfortable in his mouth.

Ben crept forward, aware that his feet did not want to move, but forcing them on anyway, knowing if he did not look now he would never feel strong enough to enter this room again. He kicked something in the darkness, a small hard item. Bottles clinked joylessly at his feet.

"Time to get up…it's past lunch time."

By now he was certain the room was empty – it felt empty, smelled empty, even sounded empty in the way that his voice died as soon as it left his lips. As his hand fell onto the pillows lined up along the top of his mother's bed, propped haphazardly against the quilted headboard, he fully expected to feel no head resting upon them, no hair spread out across the soft material…He stared down at his hands as they clutched one of the pillows, not quite understanding when or why he had picked it up. His fists clenched inside the puffy mass, fingers straining to meet. The joints of his fingers and wrists felt sore.

"Mother." It was not a question; nor was it a request; not even a cry for help. It was a word, just a word; and one that meant less every time he said it. He put the pillow back on the bed and took a step backwards, as if denying something he was barely able to grasp.

Slowly, he turned away and left the room, closing the door firmly behind him.

Ben ate a late lunch that day. There was not much in the fridge, so he did the best he could with what he found in the cupboards – a few slices of bread, some stale cheese, half a jar of pickled onions. Not once did it cross his mind to call anyone, the police or other authorities; the absence of his mother was not a problem, nor did it seem like something he should expend much energy worrying about.

He washed the dishes and put away the plate and cutlery he had used during his meal. His hands were as steady as wooden boards; he was not missing his medication at all. Had his mother been forcing him to take it so she could manage him better? If that were the case, he was glad she had vanished. It was unfair for her to attempt to manipulate his emotions in that way, particularly when it was she who seemed unable to cope with his father's leaving.

"I'm all alone now," he said, and the words tasted good: sweet and somehow bitter on his tongue. But that bitterness was not unpleasant, it was strangely rewarding in a way that the chalky little pills could never be. "*Aaaaaaalllllllll* alone." He giggled, and jerked in shock at the sound and shape of his own voice as it wormed around and into the folds of his ears.

Ben watched the shows on television his mother never allowed – cop shows and comedies deemed unsuitable for his nervous disposition. The sound of his own laughter was like a balm; the feelings he was now experiencing made him tingle all over.

Voices passed by outside the window, but they spoke no language Ben could recognise. He listened to the alien words, the garbled phrases, until they were well out of earshot.

Time passed. He stayed up late and ate the rest of the food he found in the cupboard. Despite the staleness of the produce he discovered there, he had rarely tasted such intense flavours. The cheese was stronger than a slap in the face, the biscuits melted on his tongue, the baked beans were like angels' eggs bursting against his teeth. Even water from the tap sent tiny explosions of excitement along his throat.

He climbed the stairs to bed long after midnight, relishing the fact that he'd stayed up past his usual allotted bedtime. Everything felt different at this hour – even the strange pelt of the carpet beneath his feet was like nothing he'd ever known before. His hands skimmed against the brittle walls, taking pleasure from the raised pattern of the wallpaper, a vivid design he'd not noticed until now.

When he went to the toilet it felt as if he were crapping a rainbow.

Once in his room, stationed like a sniper at the window, he stared at the old dining chair along the street. It was in exactly the same spot it had occupied the previous two nights, but this time something was different. Tonight, instead of retaining the rumour of a recent presence, the chair was occupied.

His mother sat motionless in her creased nightdress, spine held stiff and straight against the wooden back of the chair, as if held suspended in either the dull spotlight of the moon or the unflinching gaze of a streetlight. A mute performer upon a strange stage, awaiting direction; her hands were clasped, unmoving, in her narrow lap, and her arms were pressed tightly against the sides of her rigid body. She did not move. Even her feet remained flat on the ground, as if glued or nailed in place. The exposed skin of her forearms and legs was stippled with what looked like henna tattoos – thin black lines and splashes tracing the hidden routes of her veins.

If he allowed himself, Ben could imagine she was stuck there, lashed into a strict sitting position by invisible ropes; but he did not want to think such troubling thoughts. Instead, he simply watched his mother's terrible baggy face, peered into the bottomless holes of her eyes, and watched her weep black tears for something held just out of reach – possibly by Ben's father, or perhaps, he suddenly understood, even by Ben himself.

Quietly, patiently, Ben sat at the window, waiting to see what would happen when finally she tried to stand.

Truth Hurts

There were no sunrises for Cal, because every sunrise was another lie. It said today was a new day, and everything would be different. But there were no new days in Cal's life; everything was the same, and each morning was just a continuation of the day before.

He was surrounded by lies and untruths; attacked from all sides by tiny dishonesties.

Like the way this woman, Barbara, thought he felt about her.

Cal looked at her across the table, paying close attention to her eyes. They were so clear, so untainted by lies that he knew he was making the right decision. He had to be honest with her, just as he had to be honest with everyone else. It was his burden, his penance for an unspecified crime: to be honest at all costs.

"Listen, Barbara. I need to tell you something."

She smiled, took a sip of espresso, leaving a smear of dark red lipstick on the lip of the tiny white cup.

"You're not going to like it, but I can only hope you appreciate me telling the truth." It was a line he'd used before, many times; too many to count. Each word, every pause and nuance, was part of something so much bigger than them both.

"What is it, Cal? You know you can tell me anything." That smile again, along with the flash of perfect white teeth, the way her cheeks dimpled near the edges of her mouth.

"I can't see you anymore."

The smile froze in place.

"This isn't working for me. I like you, but I could never love you." He heard the words but felt removed from them, like an actor reciting lines. "You have a lovely smile and a pleasant manner, but ultimately there's nothing to you beyond the picture. I like the way you fuck and I could get used to those long legs wrapped around me, but other than that there's no reason for us to continue."

Her left arm twitched on the table top, catching a wineglass and sending it off on a short journey to the floor. Glass smashed. People stared, their quiet lunches interrupted by a sudden domestic drama.

"I just needed to be honest."

Her face crumpled. That's what it looked like: the bones softening, the skin sagging and falling inward on the failing structure.

He looked down at his hands: bitten fingernails, swollen knuckles. The pain in his side was manageable. Over the years, he had mastered it.

"I can't believe you're doing this to me. To *me*." She stood swiftly, the chair legs scraping the floorboards, and pushed herself away, heels clicking, lips curling into a silent snarl.

He looked up, offering her the only thing he could: his utter honesty.

She picked up the water jug and upended its contents over him, the water soaking his shirt and lap. Then she walked away, probably feeling stronger because she'd taken ownership of the moment.

Yet…there was something scripted about her actions, and her eyes, although set into a face reflecting hurt, seemed to glow in a way he'd never seen before. For the first time since he'd known her, Barbara seemed totally alive.

In that moment he considered for the first time that he might be capable of making a mistake.

Just as she reached the door, she paused and glanced over her shoulder. And she smiled.

Cal faltered. The waiter made a move to come over and tend to the mess, but he shook his head and opened his wallet. He laid out his money on a dry section of the table, calmly stood, and then headed for the toilets at the back of the room, allowing the waiter to move swiftly in his wake and clean up the mess. Other customers stared openly, whispering behind their hands or shaking their heads. He smiled at them all, trying not to think about the pain.

All he saw in their eyes was the reflection of a thousand lies.

In the toilet he stood before the mirror. His face was pale. His eyes were so dark they looked black. He untucked his shirt and rolled it up over his tight abdomen, turning slightly to the side so he could inspect the damaged area.

Faint hairline cracks had appeared in his china-white skin, forming a series of bluish parallel lines above the beltline. One of the lines became a fissure, opening up to reveal a slice of red. He winced, gritted his teeth. Turning on the tap, he leaned over the sink and cupped cold water into his hand, which he then slathered over the small wounds.

After tending to the cracks in his body, he wadded up toilet paper and applied the makeshift dressing to the affected area, then tucked his shirt back in to the waistband of his jeans.

He left the diner without looking at the table where he'd

told her the truth. London was filled with such places: small, terrible geographies; the scenes of intimate crimes, of truths told and pain caused and relationships ended.

He took the tube to Archway and returned to his flat above the Givinchy Laundromat. The day outside was growing dull and dark; winter was approaching. The weather reports were promising snow. He spent the rest of the afternoon working on a project for a pub chain: his computer screen flashed images of pub signs and menus, random information he struggled to make into a cohesive image. Visual lies were the only ones he could deal with.

Later Cal phoned out for takeaway, but when the pizza arrived he was no longer hungry. He left the open box on a kitchen workbench and tried to read. The words on the page bled into smudges of black blood and his eyes ached.

His bed offered little comfort: the mattress beneath him had played host to the lovers he'd crippled with his truths, but now it felt barren. He lay on his back and stared at the ceiling, at the light bulb that kept flickering and threatening to go out. It was a long time before he got up, turned off the light, and slipped back beneath the covers.

That night he dreamed of a violet sky, orange trees, and creatures with bodies no earthly biology had created. When he woke, he wondered not for the first time if he were an alien. Had he been born on a different world and exiled or lost upon this one?

He ate cold pizza for breakfast and worked all day Saturday, finishing mock-ups of the menus and a decent blueprint of the pub sign. After emailing the files to his client, he surfed the net for a while before taking a shower.

When he padded naked from the bathroom, his skin wet from the shower, he stood before the full-length bedroom mirror and stared at the cracks in his side. They were fading now, healing; the pain was long gone.

He'd tried lying many times in his life, just like normal people. But each time he uttered a deceit, someone else suffered. Instead, when he told the truth, it was *he* who suffered. He was lying to protect them, to stop them from being hurt, *physically* hurt – couldn't they see that?

In time, he had discovered he could no longer be dishonest.

Every little white lie, each dissembling notion, caused their bodies to be marked: thin cracks, like paper cuts, appeared across their skin. If he lapsed into a lie, someone else experienced the pain that belonged to him, so he chose to absorb it, to turn the truth into a laceration he could own.

For years when he was younger he had remained indoors, thinking he might protect himself and others simply by isolation. But that in itself was a lie, and whenever he spoke to someone on the phone – a salesman or cold-caller – his body opened up, splitting and cracking. No matter what he said, it didn't help at all. So he went back out into the world, accepting that he must instead embrace the insanity of his condition.

And every day he told the truth, hurting the people around him mentally and causing his body physical damage. There was no other way; he even began to see it as his mission in life. He was a paladin of truth, a guardian of honesty.

It calmed him to think this way, and once, when he had spoken the words in a mirror, a shallow cut had appeared on his forehead, proving to him it was the truth.

When he was ready, he headed into town, catching a

tube and making for a bar he knew. A quiet place where he could be left alone; where he could drink in peace and not have to risk telling the truth.

The place was dark as he descended into the basement bar. A few desultory drinkers were scattered among the stained tables and torn chairs. The lights were low, creating comforting patches of shadow against the walls. He ordered a pint of German beer and a whisky and slid into a booth. Music played softly on the jukebox; a skinny couple slow-danced in one corner, their hands wandering as the track faded to be replaced by another low tempo composition.

"Cal?"

He looked up at the sound of her voice. It was Barbara, back for more honesty.

He shook his head. "I'm sorry, Barbara. I *had* to be honest…you don't understand."

She sat down opposite. Her eyes shone in the low light and her skin was pale against the dark wooden cladding along the rear wall. "I haven't come here for an apology."

"Then what do you want?"

She blinked, licked her lips in a gesture Cal found strangely reptilian.

"Last night I dreamed of a violet sky and orange trees. I saw beasts I could not even name. I came back because something inside you called to me; a link happened between us, one I don't fully understand. I think you might have what I need."

Cal held his breath; the music stopped; the couple in the corner sat down, embracing.

"Who are you, Cal? I've known you for six weeks now and still I don't *know* you."

More music drifted in to fill the gaps. Cal could not speak.

"Tell me."

"I can only tell the truth, but the truth hurts me. If I lie, you'll suffer so much pain, your body will be mauled in such a strange way, that you'll wish for death. I don't know who I am, or where I came from. Sometimes I think I *am* the truth, the truth walking around on two legs."

Her hand enclosed his on the damp table; the flesh was cold. She squeezed his fingers, pulled him towards her over a mile and mere inches of beer-sodden terrain.

He stared at her unmoving face. "What do you want?"

Her mouth opened and he saw something glisten between her teeth, like a nest of black worms writhing against the roof of her mouth. The sight lasted only a second or two, but it was enough to let him know he was not in the presence of a conventional woman.

"I want you: *your truth.* It's all I've ever wanted. All everyone ever does is lie, but you speak the truth. I've been looking for someone like you – someone special and honest – all my life."

"But what if the truth kills you? People want lies, they expect them. Nobody – no *normal* person – can survive under conditions of absolute honesty. Believe me, I know."

Barbara shook her head. She blinked her eyes and he sensed a kind of avidity within her like nothing else he'd ever encountered. Perhaps she was as inhuman as him; maybe her hungers corresponded with his own, and were just as abnormal.

She stood, pulling him to his feet, and started moving towards the door.

He allowed himself to be led out of the bar and into a

waiting taxi. The city blurred past the taxi windows and all he felt was her hand on his leg. His ears rang; blood rushed to his head; the world seemed to throb like a hidden heartbeat.

She took him home, back to his place, and beneath a failing light bulb they undressed and fell upon the bed. Her body temperature was first hot and then cold as the fluid in her veins fluctuated between extremes.

"I don't love you," he said, and felt a thin crack open up across his shoulder blade. "I can *never* love you." Another dry wound curled from beneath his armpit and traced a red line across his pectoral, growing deeper than ever before.

The light flickered, causing strange sparks to skim across the room.

"This is all I want." Her hands pressed the places where his skin was even now rupturing, her palms latching on to the cuts and cracks and slashes, drawing something from them. The light finally went out, casting them into darkness. "I want the truth, and nothing but. I'll take all the honesty you can give, and still come back for more. I want it all, every drop. And then I want even more."

The night opened up before them, creating a space for their peculiar brand of unity. Into that place Cal spoke all the honest words he could muster, giving her everything she wanted.

Afterwards, when finally he slept, Cal dreamed not of violet skies and orange trees; instead he realised he was human, *completely* human, and the truth was all that mattered: the whole truth and nothing but the truth.

Down

Mr Campbell had vanished over an hour ago, at least as far as Todd could tell without being able to see his watch. The boys heard his voice diminishing, trailing off as if the man were falling into an endless chasm. Just before the voice left them forever, it became a ragged scream.

Now the air was as taut as the skin of a drum, as if waiting for more cries to pierce it. The boys were all quiet, each waiting for someone else to take the plunge and speak. No one could understand the loss of their teacher. It was simply beyond their comprehension.

"I want to go home," whined Chester, the youngest and neediest of the group. Chester had only just stopped crying and calling for his mummy, but the whining was equally as annoying.

"We all want to go home, mate. That's what I'm trying to do: get us out of this cave and back home, safe and sound." Todd was the eldest by a couple of months – those eight weeks meant an awful lot when you were only thirteen – and as such he had assumed command when Mr Campbell had been sucked away into the grasping dark. That was exactly how Todd had come to think of it: one by one they were being drawn into a darkness which seemed somehow alive…and hungry.

First they'd lost Chambers, captain of the football team.

Then there was Bennings, the computer whiz and science geek.

Johnston went just before Mr Campbell, who was, of course, the latest to go.

Of the seven original classmates and single teacher,

only four remained. Four small boys wandering in the blackness, looking for a way out, or even a chink of light to guide them. The school trip had turned into a nightmare and Todd understood at some level, in the part of him that always seemed so grown up, it was all Mr Campbell's fault. Why had they not been accompanied by a guide? Surely school rules dictated that more than one adult should be present on such a potentially hazardous outing. It had seemed like such fun in the beginning, as if they were being treated like adults. Now they had reverted to scared children, fumbling in the shadows.

Water dripped in the darkness; it never stopped dripping, just kept on and on, like a leaking tap. Otherwise the silence was thick and oppressive, and it was easy to imagine strange wild animals creeping around them, waiting to pounce. Strange echoes sounded, far-off yet close enough to provoke uneasiness in the boys that threatened to spill over into full-on panic. A sound like wings – birds? bats? – came from overhead, high up in the unseen stone ceiling.

Mr Campbell had been having problems for some time, everyone knew that. His wife had left him and gone to live with the girls' P.E. teacher, Miss James. Since then, Mr Campbell stunk of alcohol most mornings, and he always looked in need of a shower. His suits were grubby, his shirts creased, and he no longer combed his hair so it stuck out at odd angles.

If he was going through such a rough time, thought Todd, then why had he been allowed to lead a small group of pupils down into the local cave system? They didn't even have the proper equipment. Mr Campbell had turned up in jeans and T-shirt and the boys were still wearing their uniforms. He wished he'd spoken up at the time, before it was too late. But things had gone too far now, and everything was different down here in the dark.

"Why has no one come to save us? Shouldn't there be a search party by now? It's been hours." Chester's voice wavered, but he seemed to have the sobbing under control.

And there was the truth of it – from the mouths of babes, and all that. For his own quite probably insane reasons, Mr Campbell had brought them down here without telling anyone. There had been no permission slips, no letters home to inform their parents; the whole thing was arranged off the cuff, at the last minute: a surprise jaunt with your favourite teacher (except Mr Campbell was no longer anyone's favourite, if he ever had been at all).

Whichever way you looked at things, it all pointed to the same thing: Mr Campbell had lost his mind, and wanted to take the class down with him.

"Just stay calm," said Todd, feeling anything but. "I'll get us out of here if it's the last thing I do. I promise."

He thought of his mum, always cooking in the warm kitchen, and how she would flush with pride and remark that he was so mature, like a little man rather than a schoolboy. He pictured his dad: long nose buried in a book, the thick lenses of his NHS glasses reflecting the soft lamplight as he studied paperback editions of the classics. Tears threatened to come, but Todd knew if he let them fall he too would be lost in Mr Campbell's darkness.

"Where are we going, anyway? It's too dark to see anything in here."

Mr Campbell had been holding the last working torch; its pathetic light had dwindled as he'd been dragged away, shouting his wife's name. Only moments earlier he was telling them about cave-dwelling nocturnal creatures. How most of them were blind and had never seen or felt the light of the surface world. Describing in detail how they groped along in the stygian blackness – that's what he'd called it: stygian, like in the old Greek myths he'd taught them last term – to search out prey. There was something desperate about the way he told them all this, a sort of hunger seeping from him like the cheap aftershave he occasionally remembered to wear to hide the other smells.

"We're retracing our steps back to the entrance. Going back the way we came." Todd kept moving forward as he spoke, feeling his way along the wet cave wall. His fingers ran over crevices and folds in the rock, and he was terrified he would suddenly feel something soft and moist and *breathing*…something like an unformed version of Mr Campbell's face.

Now where had that thought come from?

He braced himself and continued at an even pace, wondering why for the past ten or fifteen minutes the rough surface of the wall had felt as if there were letters or symbols carved into it. He had to be careful here: the last thing any of them needed was for his imagination to get carried away and for him to start believing there was more to the situation than the immediate, and very real, trouble they were in.

"If that's true," said Wellington, the new boy, whose dad ran a paper shop, "then why are we still going downhill?"

Todd felt a weight shift from his chest to his stomach, rolling like a large smooth boulder away from a cave mouth.

He focused on his feet, on the uneven stony ground, and realised with horror that Wellington was right. The ground *was* sloping down; a gentle incline but nonetheless heading deeper underground. But how could that be? They had turned around and started tracking back – slowly tracing what he thought was their original route – soon after the second boy had disappeared. Had Mr Campbell simply told them this to reassure them, to make them think he was leading them out, when all along he had been leading them deeper, deeper, down into God knew what kind of underground maze?

He turned his head and stared at the figures following him. Immediately behind, holding tightly to his hand, was young Chester, still sniffling but keeping it under control. Behind Chester was Wellington, the know-it-all; next in line was Crawley, who didn't speak much at all, even in class. Then there was…but, no. That was wrong. There should not be a further member of the group. So who exactly was that, bringing up the rear? They'd lost three of the seven boys along with Mr Campbell. That meant there were only four of them left – himself, Chester, Wellington, and Crawley – so how the hell was there a fifth head bobbing along in the darkness at the end of the line? It seemed wrong somehow, that head, large and ungainly, as if the neck were struggling to support it.

Todd's fingers clenched against the rough cave wall, slipping into grooves resembling etched lines and curves. Running his hand along the cold textured rock, he began to suspect there was some kind of huge mural cut into the tough granite.

He thought again of Mr Campbell's final lesson. Ancient cave-dwellers, pale and blind and groping, stuck in the dark of the earth for centuries, drawing the stories of their tribe on the walls and evolving slowly into something new, something unimaginable – a species that might just have learned, over the course of generations, how to mimic other animals…

The weight in Todd's belly shifted again, threatening to punch a hole in his side. Shock numbed him; his hands felt cold and heavy and his legs moved only out of habit. All he could hear was the drip-dripping of water and the constant shuffling of his friends' feet.

He stopped. Chester bumped into his back, letting out a tiny wordless cry.

"*What's wrong? Why have you stopped*?" Who had spoken? Was it Wellington, or the usually silent Crawley? Todd had not recognised the voice; it sounded strange, too low and far too deep for that of a teenage boy. The words were garbled, the intonation all wrong, as if the speaker was unused to the subtleties of the English language, or was only just learning how to speak.

"Just keep still. I think the ground gets a bit tricky up ahead." Todd let go of Chester's hand; the boy's small fingers were reluctant to break the contact and his fingernails scraped against Todd's palm.

Drip-drip; the stifled sound of someone coughing into a fist; and was that quiet, muffled laughter?

"Don't worry, I'll be right back."

Todd pushed himself away from the wall and out into the darkness. The vast black sea swallowed him up. He wanted some time on his own, that was all: time to assess the situation. The weight of responsibility pressed against him from all sides, twisting him out of shape, and he experienced a sudden fast-forward sensation of what it would be like to have a family relying on him, a home, bills and a mortgage to pay…

Feet shuffled; rocks were disturbed, skipping across the ground. Todd thought he heard a sharp cry being cut off, like someone trying to call his name before something soft covered their mouth.

He had made a promise. They were all relying on him, these boys, his fellow pupils: he could not let them down, however much he might be tempted to leave them stranded and fend for himself in the dark. Chester, Wellington, even the oddly quiet and withdrawn Crawley, who nobody could really get close to because he was so shy and awkward and introverted.

Todd returned to the spot he had recently vacated. Only a single figure remained standing against the wall: not much more than a thin, dim outline whose extremities seemed unbalanced or disproportionate. He reached out his hand, and what grasped it was colder than ice, colder than the deep dark sea, and seemed to possess far too many boneless fingers.

"Chester? *Is that you, Chester?*" The desperation in his voice was nauseating. He knew the wordless answer before it even came.

Someone giggled; the chill grip on his hand tightened; water drip-dripped all around him like an insane percussive accompaniment to his dumb terror. When the figure finally loomed forward, peeling away from the wall and flopping jerkily towards him, its huge flat face heaving into view, Todd was reminded of cold tripe on a meagre platter; of the stench of an empty room opened up after being sealed for decades; of the eerie non-sound a stone makes when it is dropped into a bottomless shaft.

Then the slope beneath his feet grew suddenly steeper, and all he knew was the dizzying sensation of descent.

It struck him right then, in an exquisite timeless moment, that all they had really learned on this outing – under the expert tutelage of Mr Campbell – was how to die alone.

(This one could only ever be for Mr Campbell, who taught us all about the dark)

Sounds Weird

Money was tight that summer. I'd just changed jobs after a disastrous period working in a furniture warehouse, where I'd been escorted off the premises for various disciplinary miss-steps including a regrettable late-night incident involving the managing director's daughter and a crate of cheap white wine.

Because of my reduced earnings, I was forced to move out of the two-bedroom flat I'd been renting for more than a year and find cheaper accommodation. The result of this search was a grubby little studio in a rundown suburb located a mile or so to the west of the city.

My first night in the new digs was tiring. I kept hearing mice scurrying about under the floorboards and the central heating system was old and cantankerous: the sound of the pipes as they expanded and deformed from the passage of hot water was not unlike the low whining of injured dogs.

Unable to sleep, I decided to tidy the flat and put away my meagre belongings in some kind of order. I wiped down the shelves, brushed dust from the windowsill and cleaned out the drawers of the dresser I'd inherited as part of the deal.

It was in the bottom drawer where I found the plastic carrier bag.

I grabbed the bag and took it to the bed. It was one of those thin blue ones, the cheap kind given away in small shops and food markets. Grabbing the bottom corners of the bag, I upended it and let the contents fall out onto my bed. Then, crumpling the bag in my fist and tossing it into the waste basket, I inspected my haul.

On the duvet lay four items: a back issue of a film magazine I hadn't read in years, a packet of condoms (unopened), a bent foil sheet of paracetamol tablets (opened; five capsules remaining) and a personal MP3 player (still boxed; one of the cardboard flaps torn and the clear plastic window crumpled).

I threw everything away except the MP3 player. I'd never had the money to afford to own one, and the idea of walking around with my own personal soundtrack held a certain egotistic appeal.

Opening the box, I inspected the contents and found them intact. There was, of course, the player itself, along with a set of small black ear buds and two USB leads meant for connecting to a computer.

Ah. A computer.

This was where my plan of constant musical accompaniment fell down. I didn't have a computer…but I knew a woman who did. Unless she'd sold it to buy drugs. I was due to meet my friend Tina the following afternoon, and she owned a compact laptop someone had given her in exchange for a blowjob. The hardware was stolen – of course it was – but Tina was that kind of girl.

I took a closer look at the sleek black piece of kit in my hand, admiring the overall design. It was a sexy item; a piece of aspirational tat. I almost wished I had the money to buy stuff like this.

My thumb played across the power button, and with the minimum of pressure the machine lit up, a small screen with a blank display. The controls were quite instinctive; I found myself accessing the hard drive as if I had experience of such things. The song list was yet another blank screen, yet the memory screen showed there was information being stored on the device – a large slot of memory was filled.

Intrigued, I plugged the earphones into the player and slipped the buds into my ears. They were rather comfortable, I had to admit.

Pressing play, I sat down on the bed, kicked off my shoes, and waited to hear what the previous tenant had enjoyed listening to, perhaps late at night when he was unable to sleep.

Only static sounded in my ears, but there was a depth to the hissing that unnerved me. It sounded less like electrical interference than it did a distant ocean…and I found myself straining to hear something else behind the endless noise.

Closing my eyes, I opened my senses and reached out. The static seemed to part, allowing me to access whatever it was screening, and for the briefest of moments I thought I heard what sounded like discordant music. Then my body twitched – startling me awake in the way that happens when you feel as if you've fallen from a great height – and I realised I'd been poised at the edge of sleep.

Static hissed in my ears. The device was clenched in my hand.

I switched it off, placed it on the small cabinet near the bed, and lay down. Suddenly, without warning, I was very sleepy. Without further preamble, I slept, and did not dream.

The next day I attended a job interview arranged for me by a friend. Well, not really a friend: more of an occasional drinking companion.

"Why would you like to work here?" asked the interviewer, chewing on the end of a pencil. He was a short man, and his hair was the same tough texture as wire. His eyes were small, positioned low down on his face, and I'd already decided I did not like the look of him.

"It's a good company with a strong ethic. I also want to try to build a career rather than just sit in a dead-end job." In truth I'd forgotten what the job description was – something to do with admin, or perhaps payroll. Whatever it was, I did recall it was office based and paid more than my last temporary employment.

"Thank you, Mr Jules. We'll be in touch by the end of the week."

I smiled, stood, shook the man's hand, and then left the room.

Outside in the corridor I had the oddest feeling I was lost inside the building; it was as if the entire internal layout had shifted while I was being interviewed, and the way out was different to the route I'd used to get inside.

I waited for the lift doors to open and stepped inside. By the time the lift reached the ground floor that queer sensation had left me, but its echoes remained, filling me with an intense and vivid paranoia.

I headed towards the pub where I was meeting Tina, dodging lunchtime shoppers and truanting school kids who stared malevolently at everyone they passed. The pub was located off Boar Lane, down near the canals, and as I headed in that direction the crowds thinned out until the only people sharing the footpaths were the ragged and poor-looking denizens of rooms like the one I rented.

Tina had always liked to drink in the bad parts of town.

She was waiting at the bar when I entered the building, sucking on a pint of lager with a lemonade top. She smiled at me, waved, and ordered me a Guinness.

"How you doing, love?" Tina threw her arms around me. She smelled of old sweat and fresh booze. Her eyes shone far too much and when she kissed my cheek her lips left a trail of saliva in their wake.

"Not too shabby. Got a new place, and maybe a new job. Be back on my feet in no time."

Tina was nodding but I wasn't quite sure why.

"You still using?"

Her cheeks reddened. She nodded, and then glanced down at the floor.

"What am I going to do with you?"

Tina laughed. Our friendship had always been honest and open. We never walked on eggshells and always punctured through the awkward moments with a jab of the truth.

"I know," she said. "I was clean for two weeks, then I found myself climbing the walls and restless. It was only a matter of time before I buckled."

"What about the streets? You still a working girl?" I already knew the answer yet felt compelled to ask.

"Now and then. Just enough to fund the habit."

We drank in silence for a while until I remembered the MP3 player. I fished it out of my pocket and placed it on the bar top, pushing it towards her. "You know much about these things?"

Tina picked it up and glanced at it. "Yeah. I have about three or four back at the flat. This looks like a nice one. Where'd you get it?"

"Found it in the new place – the previous tenant left it in a drawer. Thought you might stick it on your laptop and see what's on there. It's weird, but I can't seem to access the song list – well, I can, but it's telling me there's nothing on there when I know for a fact there is."

Tina switched on the device, scrolled through a few screens, and then slid it back towards me. "Sure. Let's drink up and go back to mine."

Half an hour later we were lying sweating, our bodies bruised and our faces shining in the dull light of her room. We always ended up having sex when we met these days; it was almost a prerequisite. I'm not quite sure when that particular ritual began, but it seemed like a long time ago.

Tina's left hand was resting on my right thigh. Her ring was cutting into my flesh but I didn't have the heart to shrug her off. So I waited until she moved of her own accord and then shifted slightly on the worn mattress, wondering not for the first time how many men had been here before me.

"Let's take a look at that player," said Tina, sliding off the bed. I caught a glimpse of her Betty Boop tattoo as she moved across the room and threw on a bath robe. Then she sat down at a small desk and hit a button to rouse her laptop from its sleep mode.

By the time I joined her, standing at her side and staring at the screen, the device was connected and a file manager was open. The track listing offered up no clues; the screen was blank apart from the readout from the software.

"Weird," said Tina, pressing buttons and moving her mouse across the desk top. "There's clearly something held in the memory, but the listings say there's nothing on here. Either the player itself is knackered or there's something wrong with my software."

"Maybe there are photos or some other kind of files on there?" I impressed myself with such technological insight.

"Already thought of that…not a sausage. Just empty

space reading as saved data."

"Ah, well. How about sticking some sounds on there for me to listen to in bed? I lost all my CDs when I was burgled last year and haven't been bothered enough to get hold of any more."

Tina laughed, and it was a nice sound: the laugh of a woman who knew the score and didn't mess about when it came to getting what she wanted.

The cursor moved across the screen as Tina dragged and dropped some downloaded music files onto the device. One by one, the files vanished.

"Weird," she said, her voice low.

She tried again, and we witnessed the same effect. For some reason, the player would not allow any new information to be copied onto the hard drive.

"Just forget about it. I'll sell the damn thing down the pub."

Tina shrugged her narrow shoulders, pulled the bath robe around her too-thin body, and turned to face me. She pushed the MP3 player into my waiting hand, stood, and kissed me on the cheek. "I'm going to have to ask you to go now, Jules. I have…an appointment."

"What time's he coming?"

She looked at the clock on the wall above the bathroom door, smiled, and then turned back to me. "Ten minutes."

"I'll make myself scarce."

"Thanks, love. I know you hate to see me high, but I need something today. Something to take the edges off."

Five minutes later I was out on the street, wondering if the tall Asian man who passed by me was Tina's dealer. He stared at me from under the brim of his baseball cap, his lips curled into a sneer. He had all the moves, so was either the Man or a poseur trying to pretend he was the Man.

Later that evening, after a cheap dinner of fried chicken and greasy fries from the fast food joint on the corner, I went to bed and slipped the buds into my ears. The sound was the same, a deep hissing masking something more. This time I made out the music quicker, as if by hearing it once I'd made it easier to access again.

I closed my eyes and felt the room shift, as if the walls were shuffling slightly towards me. I tried to pick out a tune, but the music did not seem to have one. It was discordant, as I'd noted already, but there was something more than that. I began to think it wasn't music at all; it was the voice of some strange being, an alien or creature from another dimension.

The world moved beyond my closed eyelids; despite being unable to see, I was acutely aware of subtle changes taking shape. The experience was one I'd had before, listening to music in the dark, eyes tightly closed, and feeling the entire world alter around me…an illusion, and one usually brought on by drugs or alcohol. But not this time: tonight I was sober, and the feeling was more intense.

I opened my eyes, but the room looked the same. I did, however, get the sense that I'd just missed something…some kind of furtive motion.

Again, I slept without dreaming, the sound of a distant sea on an unknown shore filling my head with strange promises.

Next day I decided to go for a walk. I went to a local park and sat on a wooden bench, surrounded by broken bottles, crushed beer cans and tin foil baggies rolled up into tiny silver balls. Two children played on a set of swings, their faces sombre and unimpressed. Soon they climbed off the swings, walked over to the slide, and began to kick the steps.

I watched the little vandals until they became bored and moved away. One of them stuck up his fingers at me; the other spat on the ground and ran a finger across his throat in the universal manner of a death threat. They must have been no more than seven years old.

"Wanker!"

I smiled at them, immune to it all.

Then I took the MP3 player from my pocket and applied the headphones. I had a craving for that other world, the one inside the player. The realisation hit me hard, but it made sense: someone had managed to record evidence of another place on the hard drive, perhaps by going there, or maybe it had been downloaded from some arcane website.

I laughed silently, amused by my own wild theories.

The hissing in my ears soothed me, filling me up as if I were a pit in the earth.

Eyes closed, I rocked to the arrhythmic music I could just about hear through the static. Lacking in musical training, I have always considered myself tone deaf, yet even I knew this was not normal music. There was something distinctly otherworldly about the sound, but for all I knew it could have been created by an experimental deejay or put together by an *avant-garde* artist to accompany an installation in some obscure gallery.

But it felt good to pretend, to act like this was an aural glimpse into another realm, a place where humans did not exist and the indigenous wild life was exotic and wonderful. It might be the place where all the myths originated: perhaps the Loch Ness monster drifted through the depths of that constant ocean, yetis ran in the snow-tipped hills, and dragons soared above them all.

Here, in this place, there were no junkies, no whores, no dead-end jobs and discarded futures.

I only realised I was crying when I lifted a hand to my face to scratch my cheek; my fingers came away moist, and when I opened my eyes I saw something – something like an afterimage. For an instant the park and the swings were no longer there, the road beyond had never existed, and the derelict flats across the way did not block the view. I saw vast open fields of cyan grass, a rippling stream of smoking water, the outline of what could only be some kind of animal – but with more legs and heads than was surely possible – as it loped behind a tree with small yellow birds instead of leaves.

Then the real world – or at least the world I had always been told was real – invaded the scene, covering it all up like a sheet being pulled across a screen.

I sat there for a long time, until the sky grew dark and groups of teenagers roamed the area. Then, my shoulders heavy with something that felt like a combination of grief and happiness, I walked the long journey to Tina's place.

I rang her bell and banged on the street door, needing company, needing her.

The upper window jerked open above me. "What the hell's going on?"

"It's me, Tina. Please, can I come in?"

She threw down her keys and I let myself in, walking slowly along the cramped hallways and up the filthy stairs to her door.

I stood there until the door opened. Tina stood before me, her eyes dull, her skin pale and hanging loose on her bones. "You shouldn't have come. You hate seeing me like this." She staggered backwards, spinning into the room, falling onto the floor and giggling.

I followed her inside, shutting the door behind me. "Tonight, I'd hate it more if I had to be alone."

"Want a drink?" She stood, still unsteady on her feet, and headed towards the small kitchen.

"The strongest you've got." I sat on the bed and stared at the small device still clutched in my hand, the player of dreams.

Tina returned with two glasses filled to the brim with cheap whisky. It was horrible, but I gulped at it like it was iced water from a natural spring. "I've seen it, Tina. I've seen beyond…all *this*. I've seen through the filth and the shit and had a look at what's beyond."

Stoned, Tina sat down heavily beside me. The bathrobe slipped down one shoulder, exposing her breast. There was a fresh bruise around the nipple; it had not been there when I'd last seen her. "There's nothing beyond this, Jules. Nothing. Just more crap. Under the crust, you get the softer stuff. That's all: it's just the same, but softer."

"No, Tina. That's not right. All this is a sham. You don't need the drugs, the sex, the beatings. None of it matters; it's not what's real. There's different coloured grass and streams that smoke. Weird animals and trees with leaves that are beautiful birds."

Tina rocked, her head resting on my shoulder. "I thought I was the one who's high?" She giggled again, but I couldn't stand the sound.

My nerves became blades, turning in on me and slicing.

"That's what I am," said Tina. "The soft stuff; the stuff under the crust. It's what we all are. The drugs and the booze just make it all go tough, like scar tissue. The sex, too. That helps."

She laid her hand on my knee. The fingers were wrinkled, like those of an old hag.

I put the ear buds in place, switched on the player, and closed my eyes. The hissing sea was there, but when I strained my senses I was unable to reach beyond it. Outside of me, in the world, nothing changed. The world remained the same; the walls and floors and roof kept up their act.

I struggled to gain entry to the world I had glimpsed, and for some reason I could not quite reach it. I knew it was there, waiting for me, but time after time I failed to navigate my way towards it.

Tina stroked my leg, my thigh. Her wizened fingers plucked at my crotch, seeking something I usually gave freely but now wanted desperately to deny her.

I strained…struggled…*listened.*

It kept me at arm's length.

When I opened my eyes Tina was still there, next to me on the bed. She had taken off the robe. Her sagging breasts sickened me; the pallor of her flesh was like death; the sub-aural sounds of her anatomy were suddenly loud in my ears.

My hand made a fist around the device, and when I looked down I saw the light on the screen was fading. I'd been offered a chance and had not taken it. Back in the park, when I was alone and in a receptive state, the world beyond this one had bulged towards me…and stupidly all I'd done was sit and stare, a perpetual onlooker.

"Maybe the battery's flat." Tina's voice was the screaming of dying children; the stench of her flesh was the rot of the world – my world, the one I had chosen without even realising a choice had been made.

"Come on," said Tina, repulsive to me now. "Come on, love, let's fuck."

Her arms went around me. Her legs rose and knotted about my waist. I squeezed my eyes shut, listened with everything I had, but all I could hear was the hollow sound of my interior: a sound worse than any silence I had ever known.

The Table

It was there when he got home, standing at the front of the lounge, wedged into the belly of the bay window. Ben noticed it immediately – he would, of course, because when he'd left the house to go to work that morning he did not own a dining table; and now, here one was, where before there had been nothing but bare carpet.

He put his wallet and keys on the top shelf of the bookcase, as usual, and walked across the room, never taking his eyes off the new piece of furniture. It was an ordinary pine table, a bit worn at the edges but in reasonably good condition. Like something you might pick up cheap in a second-hand shop. Someone had varnished the wood, and it shone in the gloom. The surface was pitted here and there with tiny marks and scratches, and if he looked hard enough and allowed his mind to form patterns, some of them began to look like they might have been intended to represent numbers or letters.

Ben reached out and turned on the main light; the marks on the table top faded beneath the intense illumination. The varnish shone.

As tables went, it was nice enough, but he had no idea what it was doing there.

He went to the phone and lifted the receiver, dialled Jill's number. The phone rang eight times before she picked it up.

"It's me," he said, staring at a spot on the wall where the paint was fading. He'd have to do something about that eventually.

"Hi. How...are you okay?"

103

"Yeah. Fine."

"Listen. About last night. We should talk."

"Forget about it. We were both drunk." He twirled the phone cord in his fingers, thinking he might replace the item with a cordless model. "I have something else I want to say."

"But we should talk. Really talk."

"A table."

Jill went silent.

"A table," he said again.

"What the fuck are you talking about, Ben? What's this with the table?"

"That's what I'm asking you. What's with the table? I know you said I needed some new furniture, but if you wanted to get me some I think a chair or a sofa might have been a more appropriate gift."

"You're evading the issue again. Why won't you talk to me?"

"How did you even get it in here? I never gave you a key."

"Quit it with the table talk, Ben. I believe in us."

"Did one of the lads help you? I gave Maccas a spare key. It was him, wasn't it?"

"Talk to me, Ben. We can't go on like this."

"I don't know what you mean. Listen, I'll speak to you later. I have a headache." He put down the phone. Jill was still talking, but her words were beginning to sound like bad song lyrics. *I believe in us*. Just what the hell was that supposed to mean anyway?

He looked again at the table, at its delicate knotty surface, at the half-visible scratches in the wood. It was darker nearer the centre, perhaps where something had been spilled. He wondered if it would clean up nice, or if the stain was permanent. There were no matching chairs; just the table. It looked odd that way, somehow impermanent.

Later that evening, after eating a microwave meal and sipping a can of tepid lager, Ben sat in the dark fast-forwarding through a DVD. He was restless, couldn't settle. Light from the television played across the carpet at his feet, creeping steadily towards him. He lifted his feet up onto the chair, tucking them beneath his bottom. Glancing out of the window and into the small back garden, he watched the bushes sway like drunken line-dancers in the wind.

Bored, he pressed pause on the DVD remote control. On the screen, a Japanese warrior ceased mid-swing with his sword, cutting the air. Ben glanced to his left, towards the dark bay window, and saw someone sitting at the table. There were four of them, gathered around as if waiting for a meal. They all stared across the top of the table, not really at each other – just into the air above the middle of the table, where the darkness seemed somehow pinched or folded.

Ben did not feel afraid. He stared at them: a man, a woman, two children – a boy and a girl. They all had dark hair, pale faces: they looked vaguely oriental. He could not make out much more regarding their features because of the darkness and the fact that their faces looked smudged, like paints running together. None of the people moved; they all stared at the same point above the centre of the table.

The air was still. Ben could not even hear his own breathing. He was afraid to look away from the family –

yes, of course, that was it: they were a family. He stared at them for what felt like a long time but was probably only the space of a few minutes. He did not blink. Then, finally, he was able to tear his gaze away from the group. He glanced at the door leading out to the hall, at the silent warrior on the TV screen, and when he looked back at the table they were gone. Gone, but still there, under the surface – he could still make out the way the darkness clung to them, like old sheets.

Ben turned off the television, got out of the chair, and climbed the stairs to bed. Even though he could no longer see them he knew the four figures were still there, sitting silently at the table, and the thought comforted him. He thought about them as he drifted off to sleep, and was puzzled to realise that he could not recall what they looked like.

He dreamt of his mother, sitting in an old dining chair at the roadside – perhaps a chair that had once belonged with the table in his lounge. The street was empty; the houses were all derelict. There were black marks on his mother's skin, thick scrawls and curlicues across her face and arms. Her eyes were open. She was crying, but silently. After a while he realised she was tied to the chair and unable – rather than unwilling – to move.

#

The next day he rang his friends and asked each of them if they had helped Jill with the table. None of them knew anything about it – or that was what they claimed. The whole thing was a mystery. He began to doubt Jill had arranged delivery of the table. It was as if it had simply appeared in his house, perhaps summoned by some obscure need.

Just before lunch, when he was thinking about going out for a pint and a toasted sandwich at his local, the doorbell rang. Ben put down the book he'd been reading – Dostoevsky's *The Idiot* – and went to answer the door.

Jill was standing on the step, her hair mussed by the wind, faint spatters of drizzle on her face and shoulders. She was trying to smile but couldn't quite master the technique; her mouth looked twisted, as if she were suffering from the effects of a mild stroke. "Hi. I thought you might like some company."

Ben stepped aside. "Okay. I was just thinking about lunch – fancy some cheese on toast?" He walked backwards, into the hall, and motioned her inside. Jill followed him, shrugging off her coat, and as she stepped over the threshold dark clouds moved across the sun and it began to rain with sudden force.

She stood behind him in the kitchen as he prepared the toast, placing thick slices of cheddar across the buttered surface and returning them to the grill. He boiled the kettle and made instant coffee; the room smelled of burning. Rain hammered at the windows, shutting them in. The air grew hot and heavy.

"We still need to talk," said Jill as he passed her a plate. She had taken off her shoes, and her bare soles whispered on the vinyl floor as she shifted her weight from foot to foot. "We can't keep fighting like we did the other night – we won't last two minutes if we can't stop getting at each other's throats."

He stared at her neck, at the pale, loose flesh. She was getting old; the skin there was starting to tighten. "I know," he said. "I'm sorry. I feel…detached lately, like I'm not really here. I shouldn't take it out on you." He heard the words but did not feel them; they were less than meaningless.

She followed him into the lounge. "Is that the famous table?" Crumbs scattered across her chin as she bit into her toast. She cocked her head, indicating the bay window.

"Yeah. Are you sure you didn't buy it?"

"I think I'd remember if I had. And besides, why the hell would I buy you a table…and a second-hand one at that?" The rain did its best to drown out her words, but he could still hear them. She licked her lips; her eyes glistened in the half-light.

They finished eating and sipped their coffee. Ben thought it tasted bitter, but Jill did not voice an opinion. She watched him closely, carefully, throughout the meal, as if waiting for the right moment to strike.

They kissed because he thought they should; it was perfunctory, an act lacking in real passion. Jill tried to push him to the floor but he shook his head and drew her across the room, tugging her by the hand towards the bay window, and the table. She leaned back across the tabletop, bringing up her legs and wrapping them around his waist. He felt cold; her skin was like ice. She could not touch him inside, where it counted.

He pushed her across the polished surface, pressing his pelvis between her legs. Her skirt rode up around her thighs and he pawed at her breasts. She clawed at his buttocks. They went on like this for a while, and then Ben pulled away, stepping back from her. He thought she looked like some kind of sacrificial offering, spread-eagled there on the table, with her top buttons undone and her skirt in disarray. She was panting hard; sweat shone on her chest and forehead. Ben thought he heard a snatch of music, just for a second, but then it was gone. Perhaps someone had walked by the window with music playing on their mobile phone, or a car had gone by with the windows open and the stereo turned up loud.

The four figures were sat once again at the table, each in the same place as before. There were no chairs – they hovered above the floor, as if seated, and held their arms out across the table, palms upward. Jill's head was resting at the centre of the table, right at the point where their sightlines converged. A crimped halo of darkness hung directly above her. She was looking at him, her eyes reflecting a kind of pleading; she could not see the family.

"I can't," he said, not quite knowing what he meant but realising the family would understand even if he didn't. Their faces were immobile, lacking real expressions, yet he had the sense that beneath their skin they were struggling to express some inner emotion – the muscles beneath their blurred faces tensed, twitching as if insects were burrowing into their cheeks. Something was on the verge of breaking through: he could feel it; he could taste it, like electricity on the tongue.

Jill stood and rearranged her clothes in silence. She glared at him as she stalked across the room. In the hall, she pulled on her coat and opened the door. Then she paused, as if waiting for him to approach her, to perhaps beg her to stay. Ben stayed where he was. The family remained at the table. Jill slammed the door behind her. He watched her through the bay window, as she was slowly erased by the rainfall. He knew he would never see her again.

The table was empty, but they were there; they were always there, waiting for a meal that never came, a form of sustenance constantly denied them.

#

Miraculously, Ben managed to get an appointment with the doctor early the next day – someone had cancelled and the slot was free if he was prepared to go down to the surgery immediately. He went out into the light rain, running beneath a sullen sky. The surgery was not far from his house, and a short cut took him through a series of identical wet streets and right to the door. He must be ill – that would explain everything. A reoccurrence of the depressive fits from his childhood.

The doctor was sceptical when Ben told her about his experience with the table. "I read your file," she said, smiling blandly. "I know you have a history of mental issues, and your mother was a severe depressive. You know it's all about mood management, don't you? In your case, you're the best person to do this. I could prescribe you all kinds of pills, but I'd rather use that as a last resort. I don't want to put you through all that again unless I have to." She typed notes on a computer keyboard as she spoke. It did not fill Ben with confidence.

"I don't want medication," said Ben, wishing he had never come here. "I just want you to tell me I'm not mad, that everything's okay." His hands twitched in his lap; he moved his feet on the carpet in tiny circles. "Tell me I'm not slipping away again, like before. Like my mother."

"You're not mad. You just need to manage your condition. What happened when you were younger – your parents, particularly your mother's suicide – left scars. It was bound to. Maybe counselling would help? Someone to talk to? I can give you a couple of numbers to try, but be aware the waiting lists are long."

He took the information the doctor offered – three printed sheets – and left the surgery, wishing he had stayed at home.

Ben did not want someone to talk to. He knew the people at the table were not imaginary representations of his own absent family – that would have been much too simple. His father had left when he was young, and his mother had killed herself during Ben's long illness. The police had questioned him four hours after finding her body sitting in an old dining chair outside the house. Even now, he did not miss her; not really. He missed the idea of a mother more than the physical reality. She had been depressed, yet her doctor had not recognised the signs. Ben, in his misguided attempts to make her love him, had become ill by proxy and allowed the woman to smother him.

It was a period in his life he chose not to discuss. Even Jill knew nothing about his teenage years. It was better that way; there were no awkward questions, no issues to dodge.

There was something bigger going on here than his petty problems. The family might be taken for ghosts, but again that idea was too simple-minded. They were something different – something more forlorn and complicated: more like the ghosts of ghosts. When they appeared at the table, it was as if he were being allowed a glimpse into another place; somehow the table linked them to the world, or perhaps it trapped them here, momentarily, so that he might see them. He wondered if, in that other place, they sat down at a table that became the one in his lounge, or if they were bound to it, imprisoned in an otherwise bare chamber to participate in a kind of enforced mediumship…

But these were useless thoughts. Like all enigmas, the beauty of this one lay in the fact that it could never be unravelled. There was a table, and sometimes four people sat around it, without chairs. That was all.

Later that evening he went through his address book and looked at the names of old girlfriends. Not one of them had reached him enough to make him want to start his own family. Even Jill, despite being the best of them all, he had kept at a distance. Was it a failing in him, or was it something about these women that doomed all his relationships to end the same way? He could not remember his father, and his mother's face remained out of reach…none of the women he had ever lain with had been able to replace these dim memories with new ones.

He took a long bath and read a chapter from his book. When he returned to the lounge they were there again, sitting in their usual places around the table. The children looked to be aged between eight and ten; the parents were possibly in their mid-thirties. Once again, their faces were rigid and indistinct, but seemed just about to move. Ben felt that whenever he looked away from them they were pulling faces at him, and when he looked back their faces were once again expressionless.

"Who are you?" He did not expect an answer, and was not surprised when none came. "Please, tell me. Who are you? Why are you here?" There was no reason; they simply were.

"When I was a boy, I used to long for a family like this,

sitting around a table at meal times. It's something I never had." He approached the table and stared at its centre, following their gaze. The air there seemed to boil, rippling and undulating as if something were trying to take shape. He watched in silence, willing it to form, but the sequence never reached its conclusion and the changes threatening to occur never did. There was just that same rippling movement; a slow churning clot of thickened air above the stained area of tabletop.

On impulse Ben took off his shoes and climbed up onto the table, his knees aching and his stocking feet slipping slightly as he hauled himself up there. He stood within that knot of shifting air, feeling nothing as it wrapped around his midriff. The family stared at him, the skin of their faces pulled taut. Their eyes were huge, straining to see something that was never quite there.

Ben closed his eyes and threw back his head, waiting for something to happen. When he opened his eyes he was alone, standing on a table in the darkness. He felt foolish, as if he'd been tricked. He climbed down and crossed the room, where he sat in his solitary armchair and stared at the wall, not even recognising his own thoughts.

It seemed like hours later when the telephone rang. The curtains were open; the darkness outside pressed against the windows. He went to the telephone and picked it up. "Hello?"

"I rang to tell you it's over." It took him a second or two to realise that the voice on the line belonged to Jill. At first he'd thought it was his mother, calling from out of the past.

He didn't know what she wanted him to say.

"I thought I owed you at least the decency of telling you

I never want to see you again. I thought you might ask me to change my mind…"

He shook his head, unable to summon the words to tell her how he felt – unable to even understand how he felt.

"So that's it, then? You're happy it's over?"

"Jill."

"Yes?" If there was hope in her voice, he was no longer able to recognise it.

"The table."

"Fuck the table, Ben. Fuck the fucking table…and fuck you, too." It was a memorable line on which to end a relationship; he was glad he was able to give her that at least. She could tell her friends about it later, in the pub, when the pain went away.

Ben returned to his chair. He grabbed it and dragged it round, so it faced the bay window, and the table. Then he sat down and waited. He waited a long time but it was no time at all, not really, in the scheme of things. He sensed that others, elsewhere, had waited a lot longer, and for a lot less.

They appeared between blinks; interstitial apparitions, locked between moments. The man, the woman and the two children. They were the same yet they were different. Something about them had changed, but Ben could not discern exactly what it was. Perhaps it was he who had changed, released now from the last thing binding him to this life.

He stood and walked across the room, stepped up onto the table. This time it was easier; his knees did not ache, his mind was clear. He sat down on the table and crossed his legs, closing his eyes against the darkness. He felt them watching him – or rather, they stared at the dense space he occupied above the centre of the table. The stirring air pushed against his chest. This time he felt it, and the sensation was both terrifying and strangely comforting, like the uninvited caress of a stranger.

A sense of complete dislocation overcame him, casting him adrift from himself, and a buzzing sound filled his ears. It sounded like hundreds of bees, or strange droning music. A moment later Ben realised he was crying. His cheeks were wet; his eyes were dripping.

Moist eyes. Wet hands.

He opened his eyes and stared at his cupped palms: they were filled with blood. He glanced at the man, the woman, and the children, at their blurred faces and their staring eyes. They were watching him now – he had their full attention at last.

They smiled in unison, the skin of their faces finally preparing to change or fall away and show their true features.

Ben reached out with his red hands, and was not at all surprised when he felt them clasped by other hands. Small fingers wrapped around his wrists, pinning him to the table. He stared at the man. At the woman. At the children. He smiled as their thin skin peeled back to reveal what had always been there, just waiting for him to open his eyes and see them.

He thought of his dead mother and his absent father, of his loveless life and his heavy, heavy heart. Then, calmly, he accepted the kinship of the twitching crimson things which even now were rising from the table and moving slowly forward to embrace him.

The Sheep
(For Nick Royle)

Bill knew it was going to rain again today.

He'd expected it long before they left the rented cottage in Corbridge that morning to start their six-mile hike. Even then the sky was dark and leaden. The river, just down from their front door, ran fast and white and furious; the early-morning pedestrians crossing the bridge to the train station all wore waterproof jackets over their fleeces.

There was also the fact that it *always* rains in Northumberland in the springtime.

#

"God, this is a bit much." Hannah struggles gamely with the hood of her cagoule, trying to fasten the ties while the edges of the plastic hood close over her face like the lips of a monstrous puckering mouth. "I fucking hate the rain."

Bill turns fully around, walking backwards along the empty lane. "It'll pass. Look at the sky – the sun's trying to break through." He knows Hannah hates his relentless optimism, but it only makes him more adamant that he will convert her to his way of seeing the world.

"Want to put some money on that, fella?"

He shakes his head, smiling. She's finally managed to fasten the hood. "Tell you what, though. If it doesn't stop, I'll buy the first round when we get back to The Black Bull."

She trudges on without response. Her face looks pale against the black cagoule. Her eyes, behind the misted lenses of her glasses, are unreadable.

They continue up the hill, passing a derelict stone building Bill's map says is an old kiln: two dark arches framing a tableau of overgrown yellowish grass and building rubble, and a battered wooden door wedged open onto darkness.

"Spooky," says Hannah, and he is inclined to agree.

"Look." He points at the uneven ground just outside the open door. "It's a boot." The torn and filthy hiking boot is missing its twin; it just sits there, tipped over onto one side, with the laces still tied.

"Is there a foot still in it?"

Hannah's macabre sense of humour often puzzles him. He can't understand why she always has to look for the dark angle, painting everything black.

A solitary sheep emerges from the doorway, inching out into the grainy light. Its body is thin, its face flattened and stupid-looking. The sheep's fleece is so grubby it could be black.

"He looks a bit sheepish. But if the boot fits…." Hannah kicks a stone and turns away, grinning.

"Very funny," he says, and pushes on. He can hear her chuckling softly behind him, but then the rainfall intensifies and the only sound he is aware of is the sharp pitter-patter of raindrops against his plastic hood.

The road bends gently to the left as they reach the top of the hill. On the right, a rickety fence guards two large tractor tyres and what looks like a smashed bee hive but is probably just some kind of countryside relic Bill has never seen before. He glances at the pile of splintered wood, feeling more and more like a clumsy city-dweller out of his depth in this rural locale.

"If it would just stop raining, we could have a rest. Have some of that water." Hannah's voice is closer behind him than he expects. She moves fast for a small person: her four-foot five-inch frame seems to glide through the grey, watery air. "There isn't even any kind of shelter."

Round the bend are yet more fields. The green-and-yellow mosaic of short patchy grass on the left is hemmed in by a line of barbed-wire-topped timber palings. Beyond this fence, several more sheep stand and watch the couple as they walk by.

"Fuck off," says Hannah. Bill turns around in time to see her raising her middle finger and sticking her tongue out at the nearest animal. The sheep blinks uncomprehendingly in the face of the insult, and then darts a few yards to its left, its hind quarters bucking as if it has been slapped.

"Why'd you do that?" He stops. The rain is starting to ease off, so he pulls back his hood to expose his face to the chilly air.

"The stupid thing was staring at me...maybe it could smell its Uncle Larry on my breath from that curry last night." She winks at him – it is a manly gesture, one that makes him feel uncomfortable. Hannah possesses more natural machismo than he can even manage to fake.

They walk the fence line, looking in at the bedraggled sheep. Some of them have been partially shorn; one of the smaller animals is sporting what looks like a punkish Mohawk hairdo.

"The *fashionista* of the sheep world," says Hannah, laughing again at her own joke. She always does this, and it never seems to bother her when nobody else finds her funny. She just carries on entertaining herself, oblivious to anyone else's reaction.

The rain has stopped by now. Bill unzips his cagoule but keeps it on; Hannah peels hers off and ties the arms around her waist, wearing it like a skirt. The V-necked fleece she has on under the rain jacket is tight-fitting. Bill feels his gaze drawn to her large breasts.

They made love last night, listening to the rain as it hammered against the small Velux windows of the converted roof space. It was the first time in weeks she allowed him anywhere near her, and although he was fully satisfied, he felt her own experience was disappointing. It was nothing she said, just the way she turned her back on him afterwards. Then she wrapped the quilt around her body to form a barrier between them.

Sometimes he feels Hannah is only with him because he is easily dominated. That and his money: there is always the money to consider…

The sheep roam sluggishly in their field, moving as a loose group and keeping pace with the couple as they walk. Bill starts to feel uncomfortable. He is sure they aren't meant to behave like this. The sheep stare at them – every single one of them watching with small black eyes. It is strange, having all those animal eyes upon him. He doesn't even think Hannah has noticed.

"There's the sun," she says, falling into step alongside him. "At last."

The sun strains to penetrate the clouds, succeeding for brief seconds before it is swamped once again by the darkness in the sky.

"Well," says Hannah. "At least it's trying." She links her arm with his, rubbing at his forearm with her other hand. He wishes she'd stop. He doesn't like it.

Bill stares hard at the side of her face. Sweat forms a glistening line from her brow to her jaw. Her skin, outside in the open air, looks paler than it was last night – as if her year-round tan has receded under the onslaught of the rain. Her teeth – each impeccable one – look false, like plastic dental models in a medical display. Her hair resembles a limp wig. Taken out of her element and placed into nature, her beauty fades to a point that she is almost ugly.

Beside them, a sheep lets out a sound something between a *baaa* and a bleat. The animal sounds as if it might be in pain…or angry at something.

Bill stops walking and glances towards the low fence. A single grubby sheep, its tattered fleece hanging like an ill-fitting garment, stands against the wire-strung uprights. The rest of the sheep are standing in a line behind this first one. They are staring at Bill and Hannah.

"What the hell is this?" Hannah lets go of him. She takes a couple of steps back, her boots slipping on the wet dirt.

Bill steps forward, towards the fence. The sheep is rubbing itself against the barrier, worrying at its flesh with the barbed wire. Blood has dyed the patchy fleece dark red – a dirty stain. The sheep keeps on making that weird sound – half bleat, half normal sheep-like *baaa*ing noise.

"Stop that," says Bill, feeling foolish. "Come on, boy. No need for that."

"It's so depressing out here even the sheep are self-harming." Hannah laughs again at her own joke, but nervously. "Jesus, Bill – stop it from doing that, would you? It's gross."

The sky is still dark, but shafts of sunlight attempt to pierce its armour here and there, creating bright slashes.

Bill squints at the great dark clouds, imagining the vastness of space above them, and then returns his attention to the sheep.

Its fleece – or what remains of it – is now almost entirely red. The sheep is still rubbing its body against the barbed wire, and each of the barbs has snagged either a lump of flesh or a hank of red-matted wool. At least the sheep has stopped making that awful sound, but its fellows are still standing behind it in silent encouragement. The line they form is almost regimented, as if this is part of some bizarre ritual and their role in events is simply to stand and watch.

"Oh, please…stop it, would you? Just stop it."

The sheep carries on mutilating itself against the wire. By now the barbs have dug right into its side, tearing away hunks of meat to reveal the wetness beneath. Blood flows freely along its hide, down its stiff little legs, and splashes the wet grass.

"I'm going." Hannah starts to walk away, heading forward in the direction of the castle they will eventually reach if Bill's map-reading skills aren't as bad as she clearly expects them to be. He watches her narrow back as she quickly puts some distance between herself and this horrible sight.

The sheep keeps rubbing, rubbing – Bill is unable to move away. The sky and the clouds press down on him. He feels for some reason as if he should stay here and watch until the sheep is done. Walking away would be an insult. This creature is baring itself to him, opening up its body to display a secret, so the least he can do is observe until the end.

The other sheep watch in silence. But now, instead of

staring at the lone sheep, they are watching Bill. Their dark eyes are unblinking; they don't move as much as an inch as they stand and stare.

Bill wonders if they are waiting for something. If there is an act he is meant to perform; his part of the ritual.

Finally the mad sheep sags against the fence. There is a wide rent in its side, and a curl of intestine bulges from the wound, like an extreme hernia. The fence creaks as the sheep leans all of its weight against the flimsy structure, but the boundary holds. The other sheep remain there for a second more, and then, one by one, they turn away and head to different parts of the field. Shortly there is just him and the lacerated sheep. The animal makes no sound, but it keeps staring at him. It stares and stares, and at last Bill realises it must be dead.

He turns away and walks after Hannah. This entire event has been strange, like something from a nightmare, but now he is afraid. The death of the sheep feels like the beginning of something – as if a rite has been performed, and whatever was summoned is now abroad, walking the rain-flattened fields and the narrow lanes, looking for someone to blame.

To blame for what?

His mind is reeling; his thoughts make little sense.

The death of one of its minions?

This is getting silly – no, it has moved beyond silly, and is now becoming worrying. He struggles to keep hold of his natural optimism. It is as if Hannah's viewpoint has clouded his emotions, and is forcing him to see the things she does, *feel* the way she does.

Hannah is nowhere in sight. The lane cuts a straight line between the fields, but he can see nobody walking ahead of him. It is as if she's vanished – or perhaps run off into one of the fields, trying to escape him and his effete urbanite demeanour. He remembers last night, when she lay there with her back to him; and the sound of her breathing as she pretended to sleep.

The rain starts up again, drizzle at first but then turning to proper rainfall. He thinks about pulling up his hood but for some reason the idea of getting soaked appeals to him. Let it rain: he can put up with more discomfort than everyone thinks. He isn't the weed people make him out to be; he is a self-made businessman with a six-figure income. You have to possess some strength of character to survive in the world of corporate buy-outs and low men in identikit suits.

"Hannah!" His voice is swallowed by the lowering sky. Even if she is in earshot, she will never hear him calling her name. He begins to run. Not too fast, just jogging pace. Because if he increases his speed much more than this, he might be forced to face the possibility he is on the verge of panic.

The cold rain keeps him switched on; his cheeks sting, his eyes hurt. Once he starts to breathe heavily, and realises there is little point in running, he slows again to walking pace.

Hannah is not here. She has gone…somewhere else. Somehow she has managed to slip away, and perhaps she is now on her way back to the cottage, where she'll make coffee and put on the television so she can drown out all thoughts of Bill.

Well, he thinks. *Fuck her. Fuck you, Hannah. This is it. It's the end. I can't do this any more.*

Somewhere deep inside he accepts that he is lying to

himself, but still it feels good to pretend he is dumping her. He will enjoy her sudden realisation that the money supply is being cut off for good.

He stops walking and turns around, trying to see if he can spot her in one of the fields. Maybe she's gone for a piss, or is hiding just to wind him up. She likes to play little jokes, even when her audience is unresponsive to her kind of games. He half expects to see her lying down on the wet grass, or squatting behind one of the stunted little bushes dotted like watchers throughout the landscape.

The sky near the horizon is so close to the ground it looks like a barrier coming down; all he can see is a thin slit of gauzy greyness between earth and cloud, a narrow passage through which anything could slip unnoticed.

When Bill looks behind him the sheep are standing on his side of the fence. There is no gate. It's as if they've just appeared there, stalking him.

The lane is blocked by a wall of grubby woollen flanks, cold staring eyes and hard little hooves. They stand in lines four or five deep – he could have sworn there were fewer of them back in the field, watching the other sheep's slow ritual suicide; but now there are at least a hundred of the critters, and they are standing right behind him.

Was that what he witnessed back there, some kind of deliberate animal suicide? Is there a type of weird country virus – a sheep version of Mad Cow Disease – that forces them to do this to themselves?

Jesus. It's almost funny – might have been if it were not for the silent animals, all of them watching him, waiting for his next move. Funny in the way Hannah's jokes often are: cruel and hurtful and just the slightest bit unnerving.

The sheep watch him impassively, yet with a cruel

intelligence. He watches them back, afraid to move in case he spooks them. He's scared of a bunch of sheep – the very idea is absurd, yet it is true. He is terrified.

Then he sees what they've brought him.

The offering.

Because that's exactly what this is: an offering or devotion, like votive candles on a church alter or wilting flowers left beside a loved one's grave.

A small, ragged shape in the front rank of livestock is even now being pushed forward. The others are pressing against it with their red-smeared noses, kicking at it with their cloven feet. He sees something pink and sopping, staining the ground red: an ugly package of wool, flesh and dirt, all rolled up and tied clumsily with barbed wire. Then he glimpses what looks like a torn piece of black plastic – *part of the hood of a cagoule?* – peeking from within the sodden ruin, but only for a second. Less than a second. And could that be a shard of spectacle lens stuck to the clammy mass?

Whatever it is, this sad, twisted thing, there is too little left of it to properly identify.

The rain falls harder, heavier, obscuring his vision.

Bill stands there for what feels like hours before the phalanx of sheep finally turns and walks away. He waits even longer before taking a tentative step towards the bundle on the ground. And he prays to the darkened heavens that when he reaches it all he'll find will be the mutilated remains of the dead sheep.

He walks forward in silence, too afraid to say her name.

Small Things

Sheila had always known it was the small things in life that mattered; the miniscule details that made the world go round and often even stopped it in its tracks. Take her current situation, for instance: if John had simply thought about how his absence might affect Abby's emotional state, he might have turned up to watch the school hockey match last night instead of working late at the office. Oh, he had offered a seemingly valid excuse; he always did. But the fact that he worked long hours to help pay for the things Abby needed – school uniform, trips away, pocket money – didn't hold much water with a father-fixated thirteen year-old looking for the slightest excuse to storm off in a huff.

Sitting in the car, staring at the stationary traffic up ahead, Sheila wondered if they'd tried harder, things might have worked out differently. If she and John were still together, how much better would their lives be?

Then she remembered the other small things. The lack of affection, the way he never seemed to want any kind of physical contact unless it led to sex, the countless times he'd gone out to the pub rather than sit in the house with her, just talking about their future, and then returned to paw at her until she relented.

"Screw you," she muttered, reaching out to turn on the radio. She caught the end of a news update regarding the state of the rush-hour traffic. Looking through the windscreen, she saw enough to suspect the news had been bad. An accident, or perhaps road works, somewhere further along the dual carriageway leading into town.

The car ahead of her lurched suddenly and then stopped after gaining only a paltry few yards of burnished black tarmac. Sheila sighed. She looked at the clock on the dashboard. 4:05 p.m. She was already late, but had spoken to Abby's teacher earlier to warn her of the possibility of Abby being kept behind until she arrived.

"Come on, come on." She drummed her fingers on the steering column, seeking the music's beat but failing to grasp it. Sickening of the unrecognisable tune, she changed the channel and listened to a dull middle-class voice introduce a programme about film soundtracks.

"Jes-sus!"

As if in response, the traffic started to move; slowly, inch by inch, but this time it kept on going. Sheila allowed her foot to fall against the accelerator pedal, and when the familiar one-way system began to suck her in, she felt a burst of relief in her chest.

It was 4:15 p.m.

The spaces between cars increased as the blockage cleared; Sheila felt her car build up speed, and thanked the gods of the road for getting on with things. The noses of vehicles nudged out of various side roads as she skirted the town centre, but she did not have the time or inclination to let them out of their pens. Then, finally, she saw the familiar school signs and it seemed as if everything would work out just fine – the head teacher wouldn't be too annoyed and Abby might not go into one of her usual moods.

Approaching a junction, Sheila nudged the car faster. The vehicle ahead shot through a gap, which closed up before she could even think about following it; the shiny sides of cars were like the smooth flanks of a progression of migrating beasts. A horn blared. Someone stared at her through a windscreen, mouthing obscenities. Sheila smiled sweetly, and then bared her teeth in a silent snarl.

Then, one of those tiny everyday victories that either make or break your day: a dark-coloured car with a dusty bonnet to the left of the junction, travelling on the side of the road she was attempting to join, slowed and the driver nodded to signify he was creating a break in the line so that Sheila might cross the junction. The lowering sun flared on his windscreen, obscuring the man's features, but his large smooth hands flexed on the steering wheel, lifting for a moment in a subconscious movement.

Sheila put her foot down and joined the queue of traffic, startled for a moment when a young woman dressed in running gear bolted out into her path before veering off towards the opposite kerb. Sheila swung the wheel; the car shuddered, the engine almost stalling, and then she was straightening up and pointed in the right direction. Glancing in the rear-view mirror, once again she failed to make out the features of the man who'd shown the small kindness; she thought about thanking him – a small nod of her head in the mirror or even a raised hand – but felt it was too late for the expected courtesy: the moment, brief as it was, had passed.

The traffic soon began to clear. It was as if some magical button had been pressed to relieve the stress on the roads. It was still busy, just less so.

Abby was waiting in the car park when Sheila pulled into the school grounds. The girl's pale face was a mask of apathy tinged with an odd detached hatred. There was no doubting it: at times like these she was her father's daughter. Sheila put down her head, closed her eyes and tried to focus her thoughts. John was on her mind too much lately; she needed to quash him, to put him back in the box where he belonged.

When she raised her head again, Sheila saw a long car pull up at the kerb near the school gates – it caught her attention simply because it was the only vehicle around: all the other parents and carers were long gone.

"About time," said Abby as she opened the passenger door and climbed in beside her mother.

"Sorry. Traffic was bad." Sheila tore her gaze away from the car – why had the vehicle held her attention anyway? – and concentrated on tiptoeing around her daughter's emotional land mines.

"You *always* say that." Abby stared straight ahead, across the school playing fields; she did not even pay her mother the respect of looking her in the eye.

"Traffic's *always* bad," said Sheila, mimicking her daughter's whining tone as she put the car into reverse.

Abby said nothing more.

The car was still there when she pulled out onto the road, and she sped up as she passed it, feeling a strange creeping panic take her by surprise. She could not make out the figure behind the wheel, only that it was large, bulky, and perhaps looking in her direction. The car looked familiar, but she did not know why. No one she knew drove such a vehicle – indeed, she could not place the make or model. It was just a dark car, long and low to the ground, its bonnet dusty, as if it had been parked somewhere for a long time.

Sheila took the long way home. The journey would take more time, but at least this way the roads were always clear. Everyone else took the usual rat runs and alleyways out of town, but every now and then she liked to get off the beaten track and break free from the herd.

Another small thing, but it was one that made her happy.

Abby struggled with her hand bag and retrieved a hand-held video game from somewhere within its mysterious depths. The light from the tiny screen turned her face a disturbingly unnameable colour, and her eyes became vapid. She already had earphones stuck into her ears – Sheila often suspected they were some kind of biological mutation rather than another shop-bought gadget. The sharp, light sound of muted music filled the car and Abby's head bobbed like a dashboard toy.

Darkness began to lower across the view like a sheet being dropped onto a bed; it was winter now, and the nights were getting longer. A single car was a speck on the horizon ahead; behind, another matching spot shuddered in the rear-view mirror. Sheila's lips were dry. She was scared, but she did not know why, or what of. A formless bundle of emotions grew in her chest, pushing at her ribs and organs.

The radio was silent: it had not come back on after they'd left the school grounds.

The car behind grew larger in the mirror, becoming recognisable. It was the one from the school, the dark one that had been waiting at the kerb.

Sheila glanced at Abby, who was still lost in the world of her game. The girl's features were limp, like shapes pressed into clay, and her hands moved eerily fast across the console's controls.

Clouds pressed down from above, and Sheila almost expected the roof of the car to buckle under their weight.

The road felt too smooth, as if designed to throw her car off its surface. She gripped the steering wheel as tight as her weak hands would allow, and took deep breaths to fight her growing nervousness.

"Okay, she said aloud, knowing Abby's headphones would render her deaf to everything but the tinny dirge in her ears. "This is nothing but a coincidence. Just a man" – no matter how peculiar his behaviour, he was still merely that – "driving home from work. Probably even works at the school."

Up ahead lay a left turn through a small copse of stunted trees before rejoining the main road. It was a random offshoot from the carriageway, a pointless loop used, according to popular local myth, by 'doggers' and other perverts.

Just as she was about to pass the exit, Sheila turned the wheel sharply and took the bend. No one used this roadway unless they were parking up for some reason (usually erotic, if those local tongues could be trusted).

The other car followed, breaking suddenly and clipping the verge as it copied Sheila's unexpected manoeuvre.

"Fuck!"

"What'sat?"

"Oh, sorry…nothing, pet; just thinking out loud."

Abby removed the earphones and turned to face her mother, eyes wide, lips pursed. "You mean *swearing* out loud, don't you?"

Through gritted teeth, Sheila said, "Put your earpiece back in and listen to whatever crap you're calling music, there's a good girl."

Screwing up her face, Abby obeyed…which was unusual in itself. The girl had not noticed the strange car following them, nor had she picked up on anything other than Sheila's irritation. Her fear had gone unnoticed.

Rejoining the road, Sheila gave it some gas. Her foot eased down onto the pedal and the car pulled away, creating a bigger gap between her and her now reappearing pursuer. She had to admit it now; she *was* being pursued. There could be no other explanation.

But who was it, and why was he following her? What had she done to draw his attention? She remembered the face swearing at her behind glass; the car horn blaring; her snarling response...but surely it was such a tiny incident, a small thing that should not lead to the current situation.

The driver might just as easily be someone she'd encountered recently as some passing psycho who'd chosen her at random to terrorise, she rationalised. Her job with the Borough Council put her in contact with all kinds of people, some of whom she'd rather not meet outside office hours. The Housing Department usually dealt with those at the lower end of the social scale – the ones who could not afford to buy homes – and this meant some of her clients were difficult and others were outright hostile.

Oh, she met good people, too. Decent families with aspirations. But lately these seemed thinner and thinner on the ground. The majority of the people she dealt with were somehow convinced the world owed them a living and shouting and swearing was the best way to claim their dues.

She reached out a hand and twisted the button on the radio. Static screamed, and then died. Her fingers shook as she pulled them away.

The car remained at a distance, as if its driver was aware he had all the time he needed. Sheila was heading home, but home these days was an empty flat on a quiet street – the kind of place where neighbours kept to themselves and any kind of trouble went unnoticed. If she led the man there, this might never end. Or it might end in something much worse than terror.

Abby's eyes were closed. Her lips moved as she silently sung along with whatever song was playing through her headphones. Sheila felt her own eyes grow moist, but she refused to cry. She'd shed enough tears – far too many, in fact – when John left, and then even more when he came back to claim what he insisted were his final conjugal rights. Abby was also wearing headphones that night, and it was something Sheila never stopped being grateful for. At least, protected by her bubble of sound and visions it created, she'd been spared the sight of her father's real face.

It was the small things that mattered; always the small things. Earphones worn at a late hour, a cry muffled at just the right moment, a promise to oneself that nothing would ever hurt that much again.

The following morning John had displayed his own tiny rituals: a gaze that never quite met hers, a hand drawn across his brow, a promise to never bother her again, even when it came to their daughter.

That was when Sheila realised where she'd seen the car before: earlier that afternoon, during the rush-hour journey to Abby's school. The vehicle which had paused to allow her out of a junction; sunlight flaring across glass; heavy features obscured by the bright flash.

But why was he stalking her like this? Surely his unprompted act of kindness singled him out as a nice guy, not one of the seething masses who could flip at any given moment and under any particular set of circumstances.

The car started gaining; inch by inch, it closed in on the rear of Sheila's vehicle.

She was already breaking the speed limit, and was afraid to go any faster. She was a good driver, but did not possess the confidence to travel at speed. Gripping the wheel tighter, she concentrated on the road ahead. There was nowhere to go but home, and if she did get there with enough time to leave the car before whoever it was caught up with her, she could bolt inside and lock the doors and windows. Then, after sending Abby to her room, she would telephone the police.

Her estate loomed out of the dimness, the bay windows of houses jutting into the road like giant squared-off foreheads. Slamming on the brakes, she skidded into the estate and onto her street. The other car had missed the turning, offering her a slight advantage.

Abby grabbed the seat, turning to her mother. "What's wrong?"

"Get in the fucking flat. Now!"

For once in her life, Abby did not argue; she leapt from the car and ran for the front door. Lights were on in the street, but no-one came out to investigate the screech of brakes. The dark car cruised casually onto the estate, its headlights off, the windscreen a black expanse of nothingness.

Fumbling with her keys, Sheila managed to open the door. She bundled them both inside and locked the door behind them, slipping the safety chain into place and testing the lock. She ran upstairs behind Abby, whose baggy jeans were slipping down her waist to show her underwear. "Hurry," she whispered, not knowing why she did not dare raise her voice.

"In there. Push something against the door." She forced Abby into her room and backed away from the door only when she heard the heavy drag of a set of drawers being moved into place on the other side. Throwing down her bag and tearing off her coat, she hurried into the living room and picked up the telephone. When she held the receiver to her ear, there was no dial tone.

She pressed the buttons on the top of the handset, struggling for a connection. Only static answered.

"No," she whispered, glancing at the growing dark beyond the window, through the flimsy glass, thinking of the thin front door and the small bathroom window she never closed, not even in winter.

"Yes," said a voice on the line. It was low, calm, steady.

Sheila pressed the plastic to her ear, hoping it would help reality slip back into place.

"Society works because of the small things," said the voice. "The tiny rituals of human behaviour, the almost habitual little ticks and twitches we display in a certain situation. A smile. A door held open for someone to pass. A 'please,' a 'thank you.' The silent acknowledgement of an inconsequential act of kindness."

Tears ran down Sheila's cheeks; her jaw ached and she realised she was grinding her teeth, just as Abby did in her sleep, especially when she was experiencing a nightmare. The voice seemed too close to be only on the phone, and Sheila was suddenly terrified to turn around and face directly into the room, where a figure might be standing, mouthing the words she could hear on the line, its chunky face obscured by a flash of white light which had no source, yet hung there in the air like a phantom.

"This could have been stopped before it even began. If only you'd smiled in the mirror, or raised a hand in acknowledgement, or flashed your indicator light. Such a small thing…a tiny thing, really…but so very important when it comes to the subtle ways that society is held together."

A door creaked open, a useless defence against a force such as this; a foot fell lightly on the stairs; the flat became smaller, trapping her within the confines of her fear.

"All the small things," said the voice, so close now it was breathing in her ear. "But no-one seems to realise that added together, they amount to a lot more…more than even a human life."

She felt a body pressing against hers, an unwanted pressure against her back and her bottom, and large hands came around to cup her breasts. Then there was a sound behind her, and before she'd even realised the voice was finished and the man was done, her thoughts went to Abby, in her room, at the top of the stairs.

Slowly replacing the telephone on its table, she knew without looking that Abby's door would be open. The set of drawers would be standing against the wall, perhaps obscuring the form of her daughter's slumped body. Sheila felt the acute pain of a lesson learned the hard way.

Never again would she underestimate the power of small things.

It Knows Where You Live

Macmillan stood there and watched his wife die.

It was a slow death, agonising, he thought. She grasped the bed sheets with her thin hands as the masked man throttled her with one of her own stockings. Her face was large and wide; a pallid mask of pain. Her eyes were bulging from their sockets in a way that struck him as almost comical. Her screams didn't quite match the movement of her mouth.

He walked over to the television and peered at the screen. The actress was the double of his wife, Katie; he'd never seen anyone look so much like someone else. It was uncanny, as if she were a doppelganger.

The scene changed and a hospital waiting room appeared, with two men talking quietly in the corridor outside, their stern faces visible through the glass section of the door.

Macmillan grabbed the remote control from the table and fumbled with it as he rewound the scene. He watched his wife's death several times before switching off the television and sitting on the sofa, staring at the blank screen with the DVD case in his hands.

It Knows Where You Live. That was the title of the film. He must have rented it on a whim, probably because of the title. He couldn't remember picking the film from the list on the website of the mail order rental club, but the title had arrived as part of his weekly delivery.

The film was Italian, the technical information on the sleeve noted the release date as 1976. His wife would have been nine years old.

Unsure whether he should smile or scowl, he re-read the sleeve notes:

A series of young models are murdered while on an assignment in a small Italian town. The photographer catches images of the deaths in his lens before they even occur, and a local policeman begins to realise a supernatural entity is stalking the women from the past.

Beware the darkness. It is watching. *It knows where you live…*

"Rubbish," said Macmillan, rubbing his thumb across the laminated cover. The garish illustration on the front of the case depicted a busty woman dressed in designer rags screaming into a camera lens held by a leather-gloved hand. Dark eyes watched her from above. "Utter shite."

He dropped the plastic case onto the floor at his feet and lay back on the sofa, feeling weary and irritable. It had been a bad day: two more lay-offs at the office, Katie was upset about something characteristically vague when he got home, and there was nothing but a takeaway pizza for dinner. He glanced up, at the ceiling, and pictured her sleeping in the bed directly above him. She would be snoring, with her body sprawled diagonally across the mattress, taking up most of the space.

He looked down, at the discarded DVD case; then he looked at the screen. The film was over – the credits rolled like scribbled foreign names on a slowly spinning rolodex, the soundtrack consisted of some kind of sleazy jazz score. He wished it were true. He wished someone would come and kill her. A man in black leather gloves and a mask. A hit-and-run driver. A mugger. Some random kid with a knife.

He reached for the main remote and turned off the television. The DVD player continued to run, but he left it that way as he got to his feet and left the room.

Upstairs, he could hear Katie snoring as he stood outside the bedroom door. He was filled with revulsion. He considered sleeping in the spare room, but knew she'd be annoyed with him in the morning if he did – she needed him there, beside her, so she could feel safe in her sleep.

Macmillan entered the room and began to undress. He kept his back turned towards the bed; he didn't want to see her skinny body on top of the covers, her nightdress pulled up to expose the scrawny thighs, the hair like yellow wire on the pillow.

As he took off his work clothes and put on his sleep shorts, he was aware of his belly hanging down near his crotch, the way his muscles had gone flaccid, the marks and blemishes on his middle-aged skin. He could no longer remember being young; he was old, had always been old.

When he slid into the bed beside her he touched her leg with his foot. She stirred, moaned, and repositioned herself, moving away from him. The room was dark, but not dark enough. Streetlight seeped through the gap in the curtains. Shadows scuttled across the walls.

Macmillan turned towards his wife, shifting onto his right side. He stared at the side of her face and was surprised to find he didn't even recognise her. There was a stranger in the bed – two strangers, side by side.

"What happened?" The words sounded weak and empty. "What happened to us?" He groped for meaning, but none came. So he turned onto his back and stared at the ceiling.

His dream was accompanied by the jazzy tune from the film. He was standing over the bed, holding an empty DVD case. Katie slept with her eyes open. The man in the black leather mask and gloves entered the room and sat down on the edge of the bed. He was holding one of Katie's stockings. The man did not move; he was waiting for instructions.

The jazz music soared.

There was the impression of people watching – an unseen audience perched on the front edges of their seats, willing the action to happen.

"Do it," said Macmillan, nodding.

The man in the mask nodded in return, and then he shuffled over on the bed and wrapped the stocking around Katie's throat, pulling it tight. The material bit into her white flesh, making a red line. Her eyes bulged. She opened her mouth but this time no sound came. Her hands went to her neck, clawing at the stocking, but the man leaned over her, pressing down his weight onto her struggling form.

Macmillan woke briefly when it was still dark. Katie was standing at the side of the bed, lowering one leg into her knickers. Her gym bag was on the bed. He watched her as she dressed; his eyes closed and opened again in rapid succession, like tiny wings. When he opened them properly she was no longer there. He heard the front door slam shut.

He got up and went to the bathroom, where he dry-heaved for ten minutes but could bring nothing up from his empty stomach. He tasted last night's pizza: old cheese, pepperoni, onions.

After washing his face in the sink, he went through into the spare room and booted up the computer. He stared out of the window as the machine warmed up, watching a cat walk across a neighbour's wall before leaping onto a car bonnet.

He accessed a search engine and typed in the words "It knows where you live." He got a lot of hits, but none of them was anything to do with a 1976 Italian horror film of that name. He spent another half an hour searching, but found nothing. Even the DVD club website no longer seemed to list the title in their catalogue.

Katie came home just as he was sitting down to breakfast.

"Hi," she said as she came in the back door, her gym bag slung over one shoulder and a copy of The Guardian in her hand.

"Good workout?" He bit into his toast and tried not to look at her knees. They were bony, unattractive.

"Not bad. But I think I pulled a muscle." She stretched out her left arm and flexed it at the elbow, as if this explained everything.

"I think we have some Deep Heat in the cupboard." He chewed his toast.

"Okay. I'll check later. Is there any more bread?"

He stood up and took two slices from the bread bin, slotted them into the toaster. "Butter?"

"No thanks." She shook her head. "I'll have cottage cheese." She went to the fridge and opened it, talking out a small white plastic pot. "I think there's enough left." She opened the pot.

When the toast popped out of the toaster, Macmillan put it on a plate and returned to the table. He sipped his coffee and grimaced. He'd made it too strong.

"You always do that," said Katie, sitting down opposite. "Get the measurement wrong." She smiled. She was wearing no make-up; her eyes looked small and dull.

"Story of my life," he said. He meant it as a joke, but she didn't laugh. Or smile. She looked away, nibbled at her toast.

A silence drifted between them, took up residence on the table. Macmillan thought about prodding it with a stick, but he couldn't be bothered to go looking for one.

Finally, Katie scared away the silence: "We need to talk."

He swallowed. His throat was dry. "What about."

"About us. Where we're going."

"I don't follow you."

"Yes, you do. You know exactly what I mean…this can't go on. We barely even communicate." Her eyes darted left then right; her eyelids flickered. "What did I do to make you hate me so much?" At last her eyes had gained some depth, but it was only the threat of tears.

"I don't hate you." He pushed away his plate, his appetite killed stone dead.

"Yes, you do. I feel it every day. I can see it in your face."

He thought of a masked man with a large knife. Its keen edge gleamed in the kitchen light. No, not a knife. That was far too messy. The stocking, then: no blood, little fuss. Death by strangulation.

Katie bowed her head. "Is it because I can't have children?"

"No." But he'd said it too quickly; he should have waited, given pause.

"I thought so. I always thought so. I'm sorry, but it isn't my fault. I didn't tie a knot in my own tubes, you know." She looked up; her cheeks were red. Anger gave her skin such a marvellous lustre.

"It isn't that...not really. It's a lot of things." He raised his hands, didn't know what to do with them, and set them down on the table.

"Then what is it, exactly? Where did this hatred come from?"

He shook his head, confused, put on the spot. "It isn't...I don't hate you. Not hate. I just sometimes feel like I want to be alone. It's like...like there's nothing between us anymore, or if there is it's gone into hiding."

She was grinding her teeth. Her thin arms were rigid.

"Something's gone missing but I don't know what it is."

"So," she said, finally relaxing. "Do you still love me, or has that gone, too?"

Macmillan stared at her; he stared long and hard at her narrow face, her wiry blonde hair, and her bony shoulders. "Yes, I still love you. But it's like I've forgotten how."

She nodded once. "I know. That's how it is with me. I've forgotten how to be with you, how to act when I'm around you, how to live in the same house."

"We're like strangers," he said.

"To each other," she replied. "And to ourselves."

They finished their breakfast in silence. Not much had been said, or achieved, but it was enough for now. At least they'd made a start, and if that were possible then surely reconciliation could not be far away.

"I need to go into work for a couple of hours." Katie stood and put her plate in the sink. "I'll be back later this afternoon. We can talk again then."

"Okay." He smiled, and it almost felt real.

Katie paused on her way to the stairs. She reached out and placed a hand on his arm, bent down and kissed the side of his head, clumsily, her lips brushing against his ear. "Tonight," she said, and then she walked away.

While she was out Macmillan watched the film again. The actress who resembled Katie (only resembled; she no longer looked exactly like her) was the final victim. She did not appear in the film until the last ten minutes, where she existed only to be slain by the killer before he walked into a large black lake to die.

The plot made no sense; there was nothing resembling logic anywhere to be seen. A man in a black leather mask murdered a bunch of fashion models. A rural policeman thought the killer was somehow linked to his own dead mother. Then, after killing the Katie lookalike, the killer walked into the lake and vanished. Closing credits.

"Pathetic," he said, taking he DVD out of the machine. There was no title or sticker on either side of the disc; it was smooth and clean and silver, the coinage of nightmare. There had been no trailers for coming attractions, no advertisements or warnings about digital piracy: the film had simply begun at the opening credits, and ended after a second of black screen immediately after the end credits.

He tilted the disc in front of his eyes, squinting as the sunlight glinted off its highly polished surface. "Where did you come from?" He'd realised by now this was not part of his weekly delivery from the rental company. Someone must have slipped the disc into the package – perhaps some joker at the depot, where the films were packed up and sent out. But why? What was the point?

He returned the disc to its case and put the case on the mantelpiece, above the gas fire. Then, trying to forget about the absurd little mystery, he went upstairs to pay some bills online. There was lots to do, he couldn't afford to waste time thinking about dodgy Italian films and actresses that didn't really look like his wife after all.

It was late when Katie got back from the office. She staggered through the back door, drunk and dishevelled. "Sorry," she said, grinning. "I met up with a couple of the girls – Joanne and Gracie; you remember them, from the party last Christmas? Well, we did a bit of shopping and then went for cocktails. I didn't think you'd mind." She was babbling; she always did this when she'd had too much to drink.

"It's almost eleven o'clock. I expected you back hours ago. We were going to talk."

She waved a hand in his general direction. "Oh, well…we can do that any time. I mean, it's not urgent, is it? Nothing's pressing. It's not like I can have a baby and make things better." Her eyes blazed. She slammed the door. She had always been such an ugly drunk.

"Don't be silly." He walked further into the kitchen, heading for the kettle. Coffee; that might help sober her up.

She moved across the room, lurching towards him, her arms slithering around his waist. "But we could always try – to make a baby, I mean. I know I'm not capable, but the fun is in the attempt, isn't it?" She licked his ear.

Macmillan pulled away. Her thin arms were like sticks; her hot crotch, pressing into his behind, felt grubby.

"Oh. Right." She stepped back, wobbling. "It's like that, is it? You don't even want to fuck me. You haven't

147

touched me in over a month. Am I that ugly to you now?"
She listed from side to side, fractionally, like a galleon on
choppy seas.

"Yes," he said, and turned away, headed for the door,
and entered the living room. "Yes, you are."

She cried for an hour but he refused to leave the room
and go to her. Then, finally realising he was not going to
budge, she stormed upstairs and slammed the bedroom
door. He heard her talking – on the phone, to one of her
friends. What were their names again, Joanne and Gracie?
He'd never heard of them; before today, Katie had never
mentioned them to him.

After another hour she went quiet. She had probably
talked, or cried, herself to sleep. It was dark in the living
room; the night bloomed outside the window. The
streetlights seemed weaker than usual; their light was
insubstantial, and it barely made a circle around their
concrete bases.

Macmillan realised he'd been sitting there for over two
hours, doing nothing, feeling nothing, just listening. He got
up and grabbed the DVD from the mantelpiece, opened the
case, slipped the disc into the player. He walked
backwards to the sofa, his eyes on the screen, and prepared
for yet another viewing.

This time the actress in the final murder scene *was*
Katie. There could be no doubt. It was not someone who
resembled her, or looked exactly like her: it was her. It was
his wife. He barely paused to wonder how this could be the
case, how the woman's appearance could alter so subtly
with each successive viewing of the film. He accepted it
fully; it was part of the magic of home cinema.

He watched in quiet awe as the man in the leather mask

throttled his wife. Her bulging eyes. The red line across her pale throat. The way her hands grabbed at his arms, futile, making no impact. Her open mouth, the silent scream. This time it took her longer to die – that was another slight change, another variation on the theme of her demise. It had taken longer each time; this time it took over twenty minutes. He checked his watch. It was fascinating.

A movement caught his eye, and he glanced up at the window. He'd neglected to shut the curtains. The man in the leather mask stood there, looking in. The streetlights had dimmed to a point where they looked like etchings on the glass. The whole image was a painting, a DVD illustration or a cinema lobby poster.

Beware the darkness. It is watching. It knows where you live…

In silence, he stood and approached the front door. The figure moved with him, on the other side of the glass, the wall, and then the door. He could see its dark outline, waiting, just waiting to be let inside. He reached out slowly, savouring the moment, and turned the key in the lock – it was there, the key; why would it have been anywhere else?

He opened the door and took two steps back, one step to the side. The man in the black leather mask ghosted inside, dragging a light mist behind him like a wedding trail. He turned his head and glanced at Macmillan, walking slowly past him towards the other door, and the kitchen, the stairs beyond. His eyes were black, like stones, and the skin around them was as yellow as old parchment paper.

Macmillan followed the man out of the room. He left the front door open. There was no point in closing it, no reason to lock or bar the entrance when whatever had been coming was already here, and inside with him.

It knew where he lived. It had always known.

He walked up the stairs, staring at the broad back of the man. He wore black clothes – not dark, but black. A knee-length coat, black leather gloves, black leather shoes. Macmillan watched as the man turned the corner into the master bedroom, and then he followed.

When he entered the room the man was sitting on the bed. One of the dresser drawers was open and the man was twisting one of Katie's silk stockings around his gloved hands. He stared at Macmillan, his hard black eyes cold and unblinking.

Macmillan walked to the corner, near the wardrobe with the full-length mirror, and stood there, mentally rehearsing his small yet vital role.

The man continued to stare at him, awaiting instructions. The stocking was knotted around his fists, pulled taut between them.

"Do it," said Macmillan, relishing the scripted words as they emerged from his mouth. This felt like the culmination of a series of events and the beginning of something else. Perhaps, he thought, there will be a sequel – maybe this is even the first instalment in a franchise.

The audience held their breath. They were a single entity, a mass of living, staring, hungry eyes watching unseen from the other side of the fourth wall.

The man on the bed nodded once. He slid across the mattress, and then straddled Katie. She snorted, twitched, but did not wake. She was drunk; she could probably sleep through a tornado. Her eyes opened but she could not see – it was an impulse, a sleep-action. Nothing more.

The man wound the stocking tightly around her throat, and then tugged. His thick arms tensed, his broad back hunched over as he pressed his weight against his struggling victim.

When the man was finished he stood up and moved away from the bed. Katie's body looked like a mistake, a messy little error. Her eyes bulged from her slackened features; her skin was the colour of moonlight. Macmillan looked down at his hands, clad in the black leather driving gloves she'd given him for his last birthday. He clenched his fists. The leather creaked. Or did it? Was this just a sound effect, a post production edit?

Reaching up to touch his face, he felt only leather. But that was natural, of course: he was wearing gloves. He smiled, but his skin felt tight, encased.

Turning, he approached the full-length mirror, knowing what he would see even before he reached it.

Others…

Trog Boy Ran

Niles Reedman, stalker extraordinaire, was well and truly pissed off by the time he got home.

It was a feeling he had grown accustomed to, had even begun to enjoy, over the past three months. In fact by now he could barely even remember a time when he wasn't pissed off, and this new familiarity towards the feeling had begun, in a strange way, to offer him comfort. If he stopped to think about it, he would probably hate himself even more than he did already – so he barely thought about it at all, and simply went through the motions of his existence like a broken machine stuck in a sequence of dull, repetitive movements.

He lurched through the front door and into the hall, slamming the door behind him. The sound was satisfying, but only for a moment. Heading towards the stairs, he threw his keys onto the small shelf near the door, and then climbed up to the first floor. He was hungry but couldn't be bothered to prepare food. The fridge was empty anyway – there wasn't even any beer left in there, so getting drunk was also out of the question.

He went into the bathroom and urinated in the dark. He was aware some of his piss was splashing onto the toilet seat, but again the thought bothered him very little. He'd stopped cleaning the place two weeks after Abby had left, when it became apparent she was not coming back. The accumulation of filth didn't bother him, so why should he make the effort to do anything about it?

He flushed the toilet and crossed the landing to the spare room, turning on the light with the slap of a hand as he entered. He glanced at the radio alarm clock next to the single guest bed; it was 3 a.m.

He had sat in the car outside Abby's flat for four hours, waiting for her to return from wherever she was, and had finally given up when he realised she was probably spending the night at a friend's place. Possibly a male friend – perhaps even the guy he'd seen her meet for lunch a few days ago, when he'd followed her around town at a discreet distance, watching her shop for a new stereo.

He sat at his desk and turned on the laptop. It took some minutes to boot up, but he spent the time thinking of Abby, and picturing her on her back with that guy grunting between her legs. He was tall and dark – clichéd good looks – and Niles would bet he was a better lover, a more attentive boyfriend than he'd ever been.

Shit. None of this got any easier.

He stared at the screen, and when it came to life his hands twitched automatically towards the keyboard. He logged on and opened the internet browser. It had become something of a habit to check his emails before going to bed.

He entered his user name and password and watched as the homepage flared into existence. There were no new messages in his inbox. Since Abby had left him it seemed like everyone else was also slowly turning their back on him; even his cyber-friends – the ones who knew him only from blocks of text on a screen – were also deserting him.

Shaking his head, Niles opened another browser window and logged onto Facebook. He spent half an hour looking at other people's old school photographs, reading their bland status updates, and generally searching for something to make him feel better about his situation. The plan usually worked, allowing him a sense of *Schadenfreude* from the fact that someone else was sadder, weaker, or more depressed than him, but tonight (well, this morning actually, given the early hour) nothing seemed to work.

There was time for one last hopeful look at the emails before signing off and going to bed. He closed down Facebook and maximised the other window on the screen. Again, his inbox was empty (just who was he expecting to email him at this hour, anyway?) but the menu down the left hand side of the screen showed he had a single message in his junk folder, where any message considered by the programme as possible spam was automatically stored.

Niles moved the cursor across the screen and hit on the junk folder. The screen flickered, sticking for a moment, and then showed him the contents of the folder: a single message sat in the box, as if taunting him. *You have no real friends left*, it said. *Nobody wants you but us, the gremlins of the web.*

"Jesus," he whispered, feeling lower than ever.

The title of the email was absurd, almost surreal, as was usual with these viral messages. Niles looked at it, trying to imagine what it might possibly mean, and then stopped because none of them meant anything anyway. It was probably an ad for a revolutionary penile enlargement system, illegal medications, or some Nigerian Prince offering him two million US dollars if he agreed to launder it first through his UK bank account.

Niles moved the cursor over the email. The all-upper-case title seemed to call to him: TROG BOY RAN.

"Fucking weird," he said, aware that lately he'd been

talking to himself more than was strictly healthy.

On impulse, he clicked on the title and opened the email. He knew he was risking a Trojan or a virus, but he didn't care. He didn't care about much these days.

The message was blank: there were no words inside, just that silly title in the subject heading. Niles thought about the known scams: fictional foreign lottery wins, free cars and cash from "Honda," the fucking Nigerian Princes and their supposed fortunes…but this didn't seem to be one of those.

Out of pique more than anything else – and as an obscure way of getting back at Abby whose reasoning he still failed to understand – he typed out a reply: "Fuck you." Then, without thinking, he hit send, closed down the machine, and crawled into the spare bed (some nights he simply couldn't face the master bedroom and the double bed he and Abby had once shared), taking succour from this small, inconsequential triumph.

Sleep didn't come easy – it never did these days. His mind hummed and buzzed with plans and counter plans, most of which pertained to the on-going surveillance of his ex-girlfriend…he knew it was wrong, of course he did; but he couldn't stop himself.

At last daybreak slunk towards him like some great lethargic beast, offering little by way of diversion. Only a few months ago he and Abby might have made love upon waking, enjoyed a leisurely breakfast in bed, and then concocted some sort of plan for the day – Saturday was always special, a day when they could do things together. Now Niles just lay there on his back, looking up at the ceiling, wondering if he could be bothered to shave today, or if he should continue to put it off. The beard was making him look creepy, but the idea filled him with a perverse glee. Yeah; it appealed to him right now that he looked scary.

Finally he got out of bed and went into the bathroom. He didn't shave after all, but he did take a long, hot shower, amazing himself that he still had the ability to cry. The tears mixed with the water on his face, so he pretended it hadn't happened. When he got out of the shower, he avoided the mirror as he dried himself. Then he put on his dressing gown and went downstairs for coffee.

He thought about breakfast – he really did – but even that made him feel profoundly nauseous. The weight was falling off him; he was actually skinny for the first time since his teens. Abby had always complained about his love handles, and tried to cajole him into going on a diet or joining a gym. Ironically, she would have loved his new slim-line look. Apart from the creepy beard, of course; in truth, the beard would probably make her a bit nervous.

He watched the morning football pre-match build-up on the sports channel, and then grew bored. Yawning, he stood and headed back upstairs, to the spare room. It was 10 a.m. now; and for the second time in only a few hours, Niles accessed his email account…and once again the inbox was empty. He was just about to close it down when he spotted the junk message count. He could barely believe it, and actually had to examine the figure twice. According to the little number alongside the folder title, the junk folder contained 600,000 messages.

He read it again, just to make sure; perhaps his eyes were playing tricks on him, just like his mind had started to. But no, the number was the same. Apparently he had 600,000 junk emails held within his account.

Surely, he thought, the software memory wasn't large enough to hold so many messages. He hadn't paid for any upgrades, so the free email account came with only a small amount of storage space.

He clicked on the folder, and the page popped open to display all of those junked emails.

Weirdly, they all had the same words in the subject header: TROG BOY RAN.

Suddenly panicked, Niles ticked the faint little box above the long list of emails, and then hit the delete tag. The messages vanished, and he felt physically relieved. The tension went out of his shoulders and his hand relaxed on the computer mouse.

It's just one of those viral campaigns, he thought. *For a new film or a video game. Something like that*. He didn't know much about computers, but he knew enough to realise those who *did* know a lot about this stuff could work wonders. He'd been receiving a lot of spam messages lately, and they seemed to get more sophisticated with each new wave.

Yes, that was it: viral advertising. He felt better now he could pin a name on what was happening. If things could be named, then they were real; and if they were real you could explain them. Maybe that's why he'd been so damaged by Abby's leaving – because it was, on the face of it, inexplicable.

He got dressed and left the house, a heavy sense of foreboding following him along the path and out into the street. He unlocked his car and set off towards town. Today, he promised himself, he would not go straight to Abby's place. This habit was beginning to scare him; he really was turning into a stalker, and the thought made him anxious. This wasn't him, what he was all about. He was not a sad weirdo who sat outside women's homes, followed them to work, and wrote them lengthy letters and emails which would never be sent. Before all this, he had been a normal guy, the kind of bloke other blokes liked to have a drink with, and who was comfortable in his sense of self.

Niles barely recognised the man he had become. That was why he no longer looked in the mirror, and why he had let his beard grow so it would hide his suddenly unfamiliar features.

He parked the car in a multi-storey and walked down the concrete stairwell, trying not to smell the odour of old urine. Then, feeling ill at ease, he walked towards the main shopping area and thought he might buy a book or a CD, just to fill up his time. He felt pleased about managing to avoid going to Abby's place, and this new sense of self-control empowered him. Perhaps he could forget about her after all, and even meet someone new. Yes, that would be good: getting back out there and dating again.

"Niles?"

She stood before him, clutching two shopping bags, one in each hand.

"Hello, Abby." He was stunned for a moment, and didn't know what to feel, but then the loss rushed back in to fill the emptiness and he felt like crying. "Hi. What are you doing here?"

She frowned, the smooth skin of her forehead puckering like a row of small mouths. Her blonde hair was loose, falling about the shoulders of her black leather jacket, and she was not wearing any make-up. He realised, painfully, that she was wearing an outfit she always kept for going out – which meant, of course, she'd not been home all night. "I think I should be asking you that. Are you following me again?" She stared at him, adjusting her weight to rest on one hip, and waited for a response.

"I...I haven't been following you." How the hell did she know? "I'm just doing a bit of shopping."

"You hate shopping. You always have. I used to have to drag you out of the house on a Saturday morning." She glowered at him, her blue eyes like chips of ice set in her exquisite face. Her recollection of their Saturday mornings was directly opposed to the one he enjoyed. His sense of reality was betraying him. Was she right? Had he actually hated going out with her on a weekend, trailing around the clothes shops and pretending not to be bored?

"Really. I'm just...you know, mooching about. Window shopping."

Abby shook her head. Her eyes were now sad, and their colour had lightened. "This has to stop, Niles. You've been seen hanging around my flat and sitting in your car at the end of the street. It's creepy. Really creepy. A bit like that beard."

His hands flexed at his sides, making fists and then letting them open again. He was confused, frightened. She wasn't meant to find out about this, not ever. If she realised how pathetic he'd been acting she would never take him back. "No. No, that's not right. I haven't been following you. I've been round a couple of times to see you, but bottled it at the last minute. Maybe that's when your friends saw me?" Yes, that was it. That was a good one.

"Come off it, Niles, you sad little twat. Just stop stalking me...or I'll call the police."

Maybe not. Not such a good one, after all.

"I..." But it was too late: she was gone. He stood in an awful stunned silence as she walked away, hoisting her bags and crossing the road, where she ducked into a narrow gap between two shops and disappeared from view, leaving him with only the memory of her narrow back.

Niles turned away and walked to the kerb. The cars and buses were moving slowly, stuck in the midday city-centre traffic, and as he stared at the spaces between the vehicles he thought he saw a small, hunched figure running towards him on the opposite side of the road. The figure was dressed in rags and approaching at speed along a dirty alleyway, past empty cardboard boxes and torn black bin bags piled outside the rear entrances of cheap cafes and charity shops. A wide truck blocked his view for a few seconds, and once it had moved past he saw the alley along which he'd been looking was now empty. There was no one there; certainly not a short, squat individual with a squashed nose, a too-prominent lower jaw, and a shark-like smile that seemed to take up half its face...

Feeling crestfallen and oddly disturbed, Niles made his way back towards the multi-storey car park. He climbed the stairwell slowly, this time breathing deeply of the aroma of stale piss – it was what he deserved, for being such a fool.

When he stepped out onto the level where he'd left the car, for a moment he was unable to remember in which direction he should go. Had he parked by the lift, or at the opposite end of the building? He scanned the area, willing the memory of the exact spot to come back to him, and his eyes alighted upon something that made him question if he had even woken up at all that morning.

Three words were daubed in white paint across the grubby concrete bulkhead above the downward ramp: TROG BOY RAN.

"What the fuck?" He walked slowly to the ramp, his insides churning. Quite why these three words were suddenly able to chill him like this he wasn't sure. But it *was* scary, the fact that they had appeared to him so many times in the past twenty-four hours. Was it a new film release, or some kind of independent record label? He'd never seen the words prior to receiving that email and the very meaninglessness of them was part of their inherent ability to scare.

Remembering now where he'd parked the car, he rushed off to the area at the back of the building. Then he unlocked the car, started the engine, and reversed quickly out of the space. He kept his eyes locked dead ahead during the journey home, unwilling to risk seeing the words again. There was no reason why he should, of course, but there was always the chance he might.

Back home, he locked the doors and prepared a light meal. He couldn't eat it, and instead scraped it directly off the plate and into the bin. He felt sick and light-headed, as if he were coming down with something. Maybe it was that swine flu he'd been hearing about? The wife of one of his work colleagues had taken a hit from it, and she'd been laid up in bed for weeks. He felt his brow; yes, it was hot. Blinking, he stood and went to the kitchen, where he made a hot drink. Then he returned to the living room and watched bad television until it was time for bed.

He kept away from the computer. The feeling of dread was so intense he even climbed into the double bed, feeling strange now he was back in the bedroom where he and Abby had slept and made love and watched DVDs late into the night. He turned on the TV and watched Match of the Day, unable to keep his eye on the ball. After that, there was a late film – something starring Tom Cruise. He tried to keep his eyes open but the film didn't hold his interest. Within half an hour he was asleep.

The sound of his mobile phone woke him. He didn't know what time it was, but it was still dark inside the room. The phone unit was vibrating, making that annoying little buzzing noise he hated. He always kept the mobile by his bed, in case of emergencies, but preferred to switch the ring tone to a silent profile. He flailed about, reaching for the phone but unable to locate it in the dark. Finally he felt its cool plastic solidity, and flipped open the front.

Sickly green light crept from the display screen, illuminating a small patch of the bed. The tiny envelope indicating the presence of a new text message flashed in the top right corner of the screen.

Niles was suddenly wide awake. His heart seemed to be beating too fast and far too loudly. Could this be Abby, drunk and unable to sleep…Abby contacting him with a final declaration of love? This was when it happened, wasn't it? When people had consumed too much alcohol and couldn't get to sleep…when their minds started drifting back to better times, and the drink smoothed off the hard edges, giving the illusion things had not been as bad as they thought.

Niles pressed the button to summon the text. It opened quickly, without him seeing who it was from, but the words it contained told him immediately it wasn't, after all, from Abby. Three words, ones he'd seen too often.

TROG BOY RAN

Niles felt as if he'd been nailed to the bed. His back was pressed against the mattress, not allowing him to sit up, and his arms and legs refused to move. He stared at the small screen, at the glowing words, and wished he had never opened that email in the first place. He knew for certain now, in the wee hours of night, this was no insidious advertising campaign. It was something else, something different. Something bad.

Was Abby behind it? Could she be trying to get her own back for him stalking her (yes, he admitted it now; he *had* been stalking her)? No, she wasn't capable of such a calculated act. Part of the reason why he loved her so much was her ability to see the good in people, and that she could never be nasty, even if she tried. She was the nicest person he'd ever met – even when she was calling him creepy – and this type of thing was not her way at all.

What about a new boyfriend? Had she hooked up with someone who was the jealous type, and who had decided to teach Niles a lesson? This could be a way of marking territory, like a dog pissing against a post. And in that case, should Niles reply to the message? His finger hovered over the keys, but he couldn't think of anything to type. Wasn't that how this whole thing had started, anyway? Because he'd replied to that fucking email and signalled his was an active account.

An active account.

It was amazing how, in times of stress, even the most prosaic phrases took on a whole new meaning and became unnerving.

Niles got up, got dressed, and went downstairs to make coffee. He sat there, at the kitchen table, until the sun began to stain the sky, thinking about what he should do.

He waited until mid-morning before calling her. He knew how she liked to lie in on a Sunday, and besides she'd been out partying (or shagging) all night Friday so probably needed the rest. He used the landline; he could no longer trust his mobile. His fingers didn't hesitate when he dialled the number: his body recalled the digits even if his mind was trying hard to forget them.

"Hello?" It was nice to hear her voice minus the hate; it had been a long time since she'd spoken to him in such a neutral manner. "Hello? Who's this?"

"It's me. Niles. It's Niles. I'm sorry for calling like this, but…well, I don't even know what to say here."

There was a long pause, a silence that felt as if it contained too many subtle sounds to be called a silence at all, and then Abby coughed.

"I need to ask you something."

"I haven't hung up yet, have I?" Her voice had changed; now it was tainted with negativity, and well on its way to becoming defensive.

"Are you seeing someone?"

"That's none of your business, Niles. You know it isn't. How dare you–"

"Please, I need to know. Something…something's happening. Someone's hassling me, and I wondered if it might be someone you were seeing. Or if you'd told them about me…well, *following you*." He said the last two words quietly, ashamed of the spoken reality of his behaviour.

"At least you admit it now." Her voice had altered, too; it was softer, less hateful. It hurt him to hear the pity in her words.

"I'm sorry," he said, meaning it. Really meaning it.

"Listen, Niles, I'm not seeing anyone right now. I'm having fun with my friends, going out and acting silly. There's no one new on the scene, and that's how it's going to stay for a while. So if you're being bugged by somebody, it's nothing to do with me." She coughed again. Was she coming down with a cold, too? Maybe he could go round there with some chicken soup? "I have to go now – I'm meeting the girls for lunch. Just…just take care of yourself, and please leave me alone. Stop following me, for your own good. Stop being so fucking creepy." She put the phone down, and the sound of wind filled Niles's ears.

Niles stood there for several minutes, the telephone receiver glued to his ear, and felt caught between moments, between actions. He stood there for a long time. The pre-recorded message telling callers to hang up the phone clicked into gear, and a high-pitched beeping noise started up. Niles, startled, took the phone from his ear, but then rapidly he replaced it, feeling giddy and shocked.

Instead of a recorded female voice telling him to hang up the phone, he heard a low, breathy, ragged tone – it was a croak, really, all dry and bristling – say the last three words in the world he wanted to hear.

"*Trog Boy Ran.*"

Niles slammed the receiver into its cradle and stepped back from the phone. In that moment, it looked like an alien thing, an artefact from another world, and he was terrified of it. Utterly terrified. In fact, everything around him was now unfamiliar – his furniture, the pictures on the walls, the carpet beneath his feet. It was all scary and uncertain, like the shifting terrain of a nightmare, and at any moment he expected the walls of his house to cave in around him.

None of it looked the same. Since Abby's departure, everything had changed, and now those changes were worse than ever – they were reshaping his entire existence.

Unable to even think, he rushed from the house and headed for his car. He drove away from town, passing through estates and industrial areas, and joined the ring road. Perhaps if he was moving he could outrun this thing – whatever it was. He put his foot down and drove, staying on the ring road, planning to make a continuous circuit of the city. When he ran out of petrol, there were plenty of service stations to choose from, and as long as he kept his eyes away from the newsstands and didn't look at the CCTV monitors, he felt he might be safe until he could get back on the road. He glanced at the dashboard: almost a full tank. That would do for a while, and he could worry about the logistics of refuelling later, once he'd calmed down.

Instinctively, Niles reached out to turn on the radio…but he pulled back his hand, afraid that if he turned it on he might hear that low, husky voice repeating those three hideous, nonsensical words. Or, worse still, singing them. The sky was overcast; clouds pressed down, hemming him in. But at least he was moving, and he was well away from the curse of those words – and that's when it hit him: this was a curse. He was cursed.

Cursed.

His mobile phone rang and he fished it out of his pocket. Without even looking at the screen, he wound down the window and threw it out. He didn't look to see where it landed, and when his gaze took in the three-word registration of the car in front, he closed his eyes for a second. When he opened them it was still there, even closer in the windscreen. He passed placards and advertising hoardings flashing the same words at him. Even the road signs had changed to incorporate the damned phrase.

"No, no, no…" His own words were useless against it; he had no weapon, he was already defeated.

Niles drove for as long as he could, and when the day began to darken and night took shape around him, he realised he would soon run out of petrol. Everywhere he looked, everything he saw, he could not escape those words. Then, finally, the thing the words had been introducing, or summoning, finally chose its moment to move onstage. It had been a long time coming, but it had kept him waiting long enough.

Its appearance was almost a relief.

It began as a vague shape he glimpsed in the side mirror, keeping time with him on the hard shoulder: a small, hunched figure dressed in rags, moving briskly alongside, and slightly behind, the car. In a short amount of time, the figure became increasingly clear: it took on shape and form and substance. Before long, it was fully realised, and Niles was so afraid that he couldn't bring himself to turn his head and look to the side to take it in. He smelled sweat, bourbon and cigarettes, the aroma of loneliness.

It was running, that figure; trying to catch up with him. Trying to *catch* him.

The short legs stretched out and the arms pumped steadily at its sides, its great speed belying the misshapen bulk of its small yet sturdy body. And was that a short, broad tail whipping around at its rear? The car was moving at 70 mph, but still the figure kept pace, and it looked as if it might be able to do so forever.

The urge to turn and look directly at it was by now almost overpowering, but Niles resisted. He kept his eyes from the running figure and its big, leering grin. If he looked – if he pinned a name on this thing – that would make it real, and he didn't want it to be real. He did not want to confront it. If he ignored it, he could just about manage to pretend he was imagining everything.

Niles looked again at the dashboard. The fuel warning light was on, so he had about forty miles left in the tank. Forty miles; it wasn't much. Not nearly enough. He kept his gaze straight ahead, looking not at the road but at the darkening stretch of sky above the light traffic. The flat and lowering sky seemed so much like the lid of a coffin gently falling down to lock him inside.

"*Abby*," he whispered. "*Oh, Abby. I'm sorry. So sorry.*" But it wasn't his fault; it wasn't her fault; it was nobody's fault. Nobody's fault at all.

Weeping now, Niles gripped the wheel and hoped he could think of something before the petrol ran out. While alongside the car, gaining slightly with each graceful, muscular stride he took, Trog Boy ran.

I Live in the Gut

Now the Lord had prepared a great fish to swallow up Jonah. And Jonah was in the belly of the fish for three days and three nights.

Jonah 1:17
King James Bible

I live in the gut. Always have, always will. I'm not a cerebral person; not really. I sometimes pretend to be, if I think it'll get me something I want, but it's all just an act, a performance. What I really am – all I've ever been – is a caveman. I see something, I want it, and I take it. I'm violent and visceral. I'm a pair of fists waiting to hit someone. Usually I don't have to wait too long.

\#

This was a few years ago now; I'm not sure how long exactly. I was living in a beat-up little caravan sited on a patch of waste ground on the north-east coast, just biding my time until something interesting happened. I'd had some problems with a woman, her husband, and the man they'd sent to kill me. He was lying somewhere on the bottom of the North Sea with lead fishing weights tied to his feet. The husband and wife team was long gone. They knew enough to know when to quit.

The season was turning, summer becoming a cool autumn, and I wasn't much looking forward to the cold winter months up ahead. The caravan roof was full of holes. The walls were like paper. I needed desperately to upgrade my living arrangements but I didn't have the money to do so.

It was a Saturday morning, I think. Early. The air was crisp and cool, the sky was clear and seemed to stretch away into forever, and the sea was so still it looked like it had been painted on. I stepped out of the caravan onto the short, dry grass and did a few combinations just to loosen up my muscles: kicks and punches, trading blows with the day. After a few minutes, I started off on my run. I was planning on three miles, just to wake up my body. Last night I'd worked late at the club and had to eject a couple of troublemakers who thought being tough meant trading B-Movie dialogue and assuming a sloppy fighting stance.

I jogged slowly along the cliff top, breathing deeply, filling my lungs with that cold, stinging, salty air. It felt good to be alive, and back then I believed that was all I could reasonably ask of my existence. The roof of the world seemed impossibly high, and I stared up at it as I ran, trusting my feet to avoid any divots or outcroppings. I ran the three miles without even being aware of my body. The biology took care of itself and I was free to let my mind roam.

I spent the rest of the morning sitting outside the caravan, reading a book of Hemmingway stories. I might not be intelligent, but I still know a good tale when I see one. My mother raised me to be a reader. A love of books was the best thing she ever gave me. I drank coffee and fruit juice, ate a tuna and olive sandwich for lunch. Time passed; the sky shifted; the sun travelled across the heavens in its own slow, deliberate way.

Later that afternoon I locked up the caravan and headed into town. I had my training bag with me and thought I might go and lift a few weights or hit the heavy bag at Henry's Gym. Traffic was light; the tourist season was over and most of the locals liked to walk or ride bicycles at this time of year. I parked my ancient Ford in an alleyway behind the gym and used the rear entrance, up a rusted steel fire-escape staircase and through the glass fire door that never seemed to be locked.

The gym was quiet when I walked in. Two overweight men were dancing around in the boxing ring, throwing tentative punches with little genuine intent behind them. A few guys were over in the weights corner, flexing their muscles in front of the floor-to-ceiling mirror. Two women were working on the heavy bag: one of them – a willowy blonde with a bright red Alice band around her head – was holding the bag while the other – an athletic black woman with striking green eyes – put all she had into a series of kicks and punches that looked like they'd take your head off if they connected.

I nodded at Henry, who was sitting in his glass booth listening to a radio talk show. He smiled in that slow, sure way of his and raised his calloused right hand, the one with the missing thumb. I went into the changing room and slipped into some loose-fitting tracksuit bottoms and a Guinness T-shirt. Then I put my bag in the locker I rented there, and went back out into the main gym area.

The boxers were still moving around the scuffed canvas ring, their feet sounding like whisks on a drum. One of them raised a gloved hand as I passed by. I recognised the face but couldn't put a name to it, so I just nodded and continued on my way towards the squat machine.

After my workout – legs and shoulders today – I went over to say a proper hello to Henry.

"How you doing?" His voice was low, grizzled from the throat cancer he'd beaten into submission several years ago.

"Not bad. Been better, been a hell of a lot worse."

He laughed. "Sit down."

I lowered myself into the wooden chair opposite him and leaned back, yawning.

"Am I keeping you up?"

"It's been a tough few days. I've lost some sleep."

Henry smiled, nodded. He knew enough about me not to ask for any details. We'd worked together in the past, on small jobs – putting the frighteners on debtors, warning off violent ex-husbands, collecting money from people who gambled but then didn't like to pay – and he knew I was capable of looking after myself.

"You haven't been around for a while. Back for good?"

I nodded. "Yeah, I need to get back in shape. I'm working three nights a week at The Maple Lounge, so I've got to get my reflexes back."

"I can set you up with a good sparring partner. A kid out of Wales. He needs some serious ring time to prepare for a title fight."

"What discipline?"

"Muay Thai."

I nodded. "Set it up. He might kick my arse, but I could probably use the lesson in humility." I stood and walked to the door, turned around. "Come over and see me tonight. I have a good bottle of scotch and a craving for some company."

Henry nodded without looking up from his paperwork.

"See you around nine."

I walked out the door, went down to my car – I'd used that same back door to the gym, which had become a habit. By the time I got back to my caravan it was late afternoon. I sat outside and drank a glass of pale ale, watching the sun make its slovenly way down towards the horizon line: the terminator, the line between dark and light, good and evil.

I was feeling restless so I took a walk down to the beach. I liked it at this time of day. All the day-trippers were long gone, and the only person I might see would be a solitary dog walker, throwing a stick or a ball for their canine companion. I made my way down the cliff-side path, stones shifting under my feet, loose dirt rattling down the narrow single-track ahead of me.

I noticed the body before I even reached the sand. At that point I didn't know for sure what it was, but I've seen enough dead bodies to recognise the signs. I saw my first one in Afghanistan. All the corpses I've seen since coming out of the army were not wearing uniforms.

I walked slowly across the dry sand until it became wet and hard, then I stopped, scanned the beach in all directions. It was quiet, empty. The only sound was the surf, lapping away at the shore. The body – and now I could be certain that it was a body – was lying about three or four metres away from the white-foam surf. Face down, one arm by its side and the other stretched upwards on the sand. I couldn't help noticing she was naked.

I started walking again and when I reached the spot I crouched down to examine the body closer. The sea smell overpowered any kind of stench so I didn't know how long the body had been there. It was a woman. She had long dark hair, knotted with seaweed and sand and tiny dead crabs. Upon closer inspection, I could see she didn't have any hands or feet. They'd been severed. Then, when I looked again, I realised my mistake. They had not been cut off; they were intact, but they didn't resemble normal hands and feet. They looked like flippers.

I checked the beach again. Nobody there. Glancing up at the cliff-top, I confirmed I wasn't being watched. Then I turned her over onto her back. Her face was wide and pale and her eyes were huge, with big black pupils. She had cheekbones like razorblades, and they were high up, giving her an aristocratic look. Her lips were blue. They were slightly parted, showing a row of small white jagged teeth. Her breasts were huge, her waist was as thin as my calf, and her crotch was smooth and hairless. The slit down there looked like a gill; it matched the ones situated at both sides of her body, below the ribcage. There was a deep cut in her belly. The wound was clean, but I could see it had bled out a lot before she'd been washed ashore.

She was the closest thing I'd ever seen to true beauty.

I didn't know what else to do, so I picked her up and carried her off the sand, up the cliff-side path, and back to my caravan. I lay her down in the bathtub in the cramped little bathroom pod. When I stepped back into the doorway, sweating and aching and wondering what the hell I was going to do next, one of those little gills on her side opened slightly, like a puckering pair of lips.

Her eyes – open so wide when I found her – were now closed. The thin, papery eyelids flickered; I could see the movement of her eyeballs beneath. She blinked, but the eyelids moved sideways instead of up and down. I grabbed the shower head and pointed it at her body, then turned on the water. The shower spray made her body shiver, as if a series of tiny orgasms was gripping her. The flippers on the ends of her hands and feet slapped lazily against the hard enamel sides of the bathtub.

I wetted her body for fifteen minutes. Then I turned off the shower and dressed her wound as best as I could. Her right flipper lifted momentarily and brushed the side of my face. It felt soft and surprisingly warm.

I was sitting outside, thinking, when Henry arrived. He'd walked the short distance from town.

"Evenin'," he said. It was only then I noticed it was dark.

"I got something to show you."

He didn't flinch. He'd known me long enough to realise it was probably something serious.

"Okay. So show me."

I took him inside, opened the plastic bi-fold bathroom door, and waited for him to say something.

It took him a while.

"What the fuck is it?" His old face was more creased than it had been.

I sighed. "I don't know. Found her on the beach this afternoon. She was wounded…I thought she was dead."

"But she isn't? She's alive?"

"Yeah, she's alive. She's breathing."

"Through them gill things?"

"Yeah…watch them for a little bit. You should be able to see them moving."

We waited, watched, and saw the gills twitch as she took in air.

"How are you keeping her alive?"

"I'm not sure. She seems to respond when I douse her with water, so I've been doing that every half hour or so."

"With the shower?"

"Yeah, the shower. She likes it, I think."

"Has she spoken?"

"She hasn't even opened her eyes. Not since I brought her in here, anyway. They were open when I found her. Now they're closed. I think…I think she's resting."

"You know what this is, don't you?" He turned to me, his face ashen. "You know what she is?"

I shook my head.

"She's a mermaid. She's a fuckin' mermaid."

"She doesn't have a tail," I said, aware of the absurdity of the statement but unable to even smile. "And mermaids don't exist."

"Maybe they do, brother. And maybe they don't look like that. Maybe they look like this." He swept his hand in an odd gesture, as if encompassing the tiny room and everything in it, not just the motionless figure in the bath.

"I need a drink," I said.

"Good idea."

We went back outside. I grabbed the whisky bottle and two glasses on the way. We sat down and I poured the drinks. Henry finished his drink in a single gulp.

The next hour or so passed quickly, and neither of us seemed to have much to say. I knew Henry was thinking about the creature in my bathtub, but all I was doing was staring out at the sea and wondering where the hell she had come from.

Presently, Henry shifted in his seat. He put down the half empty bottle on the ground at his feet. "Can I go and take another look at her?"

I should have recognised the look on his face, but I didn't. I'd seen that same slack, hungry expression once before, just before he'd molested a post office worker we'd abducted so we could give her gambling-cheat of a husband a little scare. But this time, I didn't see it coming. I blame the night and the cold, fresh sea air, and the fact that nothing about this situation seemed entirely real.

"Sure," I said. "Give her another spray while you're in there."

I waited a long time before I realised he should have come back by now. I set down my glass and stood, watching the horizon waver before my eyes. Too much whisky, too little sleep, too much weirdness...

I went back inside, grabbing the doorframe to steady myself as I stumbled over the top step. I could hear the noise as I approached the closed bathroom door: heavy breathing, grunting, like a pig at the trough; the word "Bitch" being repeated over and over again in Henry's hard-edged whispery growl; something slapping repeatedly against the sides of the bathtub.

I dragged open the door and saw him lying on top of her in the tub, his pants dragged halfway down his legs and his big white arse pumping up and down, rising and falling like some horrible moon. He had his hands on her wrists directly beneath the flippers, pressing them against the enamel. For some reason all I could focus on was his missing thumb. Her legs were spread awkwardly, squashed against the sides of the narrow tub, and her lower flippers were flailing around in panic.

I reached down and grabbed him by the back of the neck. He was a big man, but I lifted him easily. He didn't say a thing, and his body went limp, accepting what was about to happen. I didn't stop hitting him until his face was a red tattered mess and long after he'd stopped struggling.

I went over to the bath and looked down at her. She was stiff, unmoving. The dressing on her belly had come loose and something had spilled out: it looked like red seaweed, trailing across her lower abdomen. For the first time I noticed she didn't have a belly button. It was a small thing, a minor detail, but at that moment it seemed vital, a sign of something more significant than this tawdry scene.

I dragged Henry outside and hoisted him onto my shoulders, in a fireman's lift. I had a little boat I kept tied up in a rock pool down by the shore. It wouldn't be the first time I'd disposed of a problem in this way. He had been my friend, but after what he had done I no longer recognised him. He was just as feral and venal as the rest of the scum I dealt with. Whatever had once been special about him was long gone.

I saw the thing on the beach as I approached the cliff top. It would be impossible not to see, because it was so big, so alien on the night-time sand. What came to mind were those old pencil-sketch artist's impressions of sea monsters, the ones you see in old books about the ocean. The ones I loved to look at as a child.

At first I thought it was some kind of beached whale, but as my eyes adjusted to the moonlight I realised it looked nothing like a whale. It was more like one of those giant squid things from old sailors' charts – what they used to call a kraken. Its body was long and plump, with eight suckered octopus-like arms it was currently using to pull itself up the beach towards the cliff.

It moved oddly yet gracefully, flowing like black ink against the starry sky and the flat sand. It had a beaked face, but there was something human about the rest of its features…big, dark eyes, a delicate brow, high, sharp cheekbones. The first word to enter my head as I stared at it was 'beautiful.' It was only later when I realised how much the thing's face resembled that of the woman in my bathtub, at least in general terms.

I threw Henry down the cliff and hoped it was enough to appease the thing that had come up from the depths. I had nothing else to give, nothing left to offer up as a sacrifice. The best of me had withered long ago; all that remained was dust and shadows.

When I turned around, she was standing there before me, backlit by the meagre caravan lights. I hadn't even heard her approach. The dressing had fallen away from her belly, and smaller versions of those octopus arms I'd seen on the thing on the beach were emerging from the cavity to wave around in the air...or maybe it was just her innards spilling out, and I saw what I wanted to, what I needed to.

She lifted one flipper and touched my forehead. I felt calm, cool, collected, just like I always do in the last few seconds before a fight. I reached out and she took my hand in her smooth, soft flipper, then she led me down the narrow pathway to the beach, where the other thing waited, crunching disconsolately on Henry's bones.

Close-up, its hide was thick and leathery. There were ugly gouges and gashes along its flanks, as if it had been fighting with sharks or orcas or crashing through huge, ancient coral reefs as it travelled through the night-black depths. Part of me realised it could be a whale, mortally wounded, torn up from some battle. But the rest of me wanted to believe it was something else.

I stared at the creature, drunk on its wonder. It was an awesome sight; it was a leviathan of the imagination, a creature more fantasy than fact. But even as I watched, its body began to sag and fade. The life seemed to drain out of the thing as I stood there and watched it perish.

She stepped forward and approached the waning giant, pulled aside a flap in its belly, tearing it apart to create an entrance. Its body shuddered once, and then went still. Dull red light seeped out of the rent in its side, coating the sand like blood. The tent-like interior looked warm and dry…and it was welcoming, like a heated shelter on a cold day. There were no bones, no internal organs I could see. She bent down and slipped one leg inside, and turned to me, beckoning with her long, pale, boneless arm.

I thought about the life I would be leaving behind if I joined her inside this strange vessel. The gym, the fights, the bad women and even worse men…all the minor battles and skirmishes my life had become; the constant struggle for meaning in a world that had none.

Then I thought again of the words I'd contemplated before and how apt they might now become: that thing about living in the gut rather than the head. There was meaning here, but it lay just out of reach. Perhaps if I were an intelligent man – a thinker rather than a fighter – I might be able to grasp it. Then I went blank, taking the easy way, refusing to think of anything at all. Thinking was not what I did best. Doing was my thing, and I usually did it well.

Accepting this felt as if I were severing the last remaining link to everyone and every single thing I had ever hated.

"Fuck it," I said.

Then I smiled, walked forward, and entered into the brilliant unknown.

It Won't Be Long Now

Please, have another drink. Could you pour me one while you're at it? Thank you.

So. How do you feel?

Good, good...

Did you get much sleep last night?

Well, yes, I suppose you were anxious.

And the money? Everything went okay with the electronic transfer?

That's good. We're all ready, then. Ready to go.

It won't be long now. I'm sure. Don't be nervous. I'm not. I'm more than ready for this. I've been preparing for a long time. Preparing mentally. I've made my peace. I hope you can do the same.

Mmm...lovely. I will miss this, though. Good whisky. I won't miss much else, I don't think.

(pause)

Apropos of nothing, I remember when I was a small child. We used to have family holidays by the sea. Even my father used to come along, if he wasn't too busy. I always loved the coast...that sense of *hugeness*. The sea doesn't judge. It doesn't remember. It just *is*.

Do you know what I mean?

Perhaps not.

I'm sorry. I'm rambling. It's the excitement, you see, the thought of so much preparation finally paying off. Maybe I shouldn't have had another drink after all. I want to be sober during this. I want to savour each and every second. It isn't every day something like this happens. It is – if you'll forgive the bad pun – a real once-in-a-lifetime experience.

(pause)

Those? Yes, they're the…tools. The apparatus. Don't worry. They'll show you when they get here. Everything will be explained. I'm sure you recognise some of them – you had medical training in your home country, didn't you? You were some kind of doctor?

That's why your name was on the list.

Those other items on the table…well, they might look a bit strange, but I assure you they're 'fit-for-task.' They've been designed specifically for the job.

(pause)

I hope you have steady hands.

A surgeon? Were you really? Well, that's good. My people must've done their research well. As a surgeon, you should be able to appreciate all of this. I'm sure you have a full understanding of the nature of pain, too, and how to control it.

Yes, yes…I know doctors are meant to value the sanctity of life, but, in a way, that's what this is all about. The sanctity of life…and how by defiling it we can create an entertainment.

I know. I know you don't approve…and, truly, I'm sorry about that.

Excuse me? The camera? Yes, they're bringing all that gear with them. It's all digital now. Nothing to set up: just point-and-press technology. Natural lighting. Sound recording is built into the camera. All very clever stuff, not like the old days when we had to spend hours prepping for a shoot. I suppose I'm seeing it all from the other side now, a different angle. Rather than organising everything behind the camera, I'm the star of the show.

(pause)

Well. Isn't this cosy? I'm glad I had the chance to get to know you a little before, well, before it's done. Before you do it.

(pause)

Your family...they're glad of the money, yes? I suppose it means a lot to them – to their lives, where they live. Africa, isn't it?

Ah, yes. I've read about that place in the papers...civil war, drought, disease. I'm not surprised you needed to send them money. I'm glad I could help them get out of that mess. Please, send them my regards when you see them. And treasure them...life's too short not to cherish the ones we love.

Believe me, I know.

The world is experiencing terrible times, times of great change and austerity. Each man must do what he must to put bread on the table. I'm right, aren't I? And during such times, businesses like mine will continue to flourish. It's not something I'm proud of – it's simply an economic fact.

Indeed, in times gone by, people like your family would've been the ones here, in my place. But these days our customers have more...*sophisticated* tastes. Can I even call it that? Sophisticated? It doesn't seem right somehow. Perhaps 'esoteric' would be a more appropriate choice of word.

(pause)

The market has changed. Viewing tastes have altered and become more radical, less predictable. In the past, it was all about blood and sex, but now they don't seem to want that. It's passé.

The current trend seems to involve intense anatomical

exploration…hence the need for someone like you, with your background in medicine.

A *surgeon*, no less…

(pause)

It's difficult to guess the next thing they'll want to see, but we're expecting this to be what is usually called a game-changer.

(pause)

I'm sorry, what did you say?

Oh, yes, there is that. The guilt…but don't feel guilty afterwards, not on my behalf. I assure you I want this. I want it very much. The last thing I need is to…linger. I always said I'd rather go out this way, providing a service to my customers.

Like I said before, I've been preparing for this. It isn't just something I decided on the spur of the moment. I suppose it was my intention all along, once I found out I was dying.

Excuse me. That's just my phone. A text message.

(pause)

Yes, they're on their way.

It won't be long now. Not long at all.

You Haven't Seen me

Trendle hated being out this late in the Grove estate, long after the working populace had packed up and gone home. It was a leftover fear from the time, almost seven years ago, when he'd been mugged by a masked stranger as he was walking home from the pub. The man punched him twice in the kidneys, and when Trendle was on the ground his assailant kicked him in the head. There followed the feeling of hands going through his shirt pocket, coat pockets, trouser pockets, and removing anything of value. The bastard even took his watch.

But that was a long time ago, and he realised he should be over it by now. Should be, but wasn't. He still carried the scars – both physical and mental – and walking these dark streets brought back all the memories with a force that was at times like a psychological echo of those initial blows.

Just before running away, his attacker had leaned in and whispered, with a note of amusement in his voice, "You haven't seen me. I was never here." The words seemed to resonate even now with something beyond their apparent meaning, and the fact that the mugger was never caught served only to underline the implied threat. He was still out there somewhere, probably doing the same to other people.

Trendle had stayed late at the council offices on Far Grove Way this evening because he needed the overtime money. He thought it would be okay. He convinced himself he no longer feared being out here, on the streets, as darkness fell. Or at least his need for extra cash outweighed the terror he carried with him, hoping nobody would notice.

But he had lied to himself. Right now, he just wanted to get away, to be safely home within the sanctity of the small house where he had lived alone since his mother died over a decade ago.

He hurried past boarded-up shops, businesses that hadn't traded in years; dark alleys opened like hungry mouths along his route to the bus stop, belching out a twitching sodium-tinted darkness.

"Stupid," he whispered. "Stupid, stupid man…" He always did this, created illusory fears to supplement the ones that already existed. Sometimes Trendle believed he secretly enjoyed being afraid.

Hadn't there been something in the papers recently about a murder nearby? Or was he just making that up, too, his mind conspiring with the environment to scare him even more? Fears lined up to bait him like paupers in a breadline, and he embraced them all, giving them sustenance.

Shadows juddered up ahead, a nervy dance of darkness. Trendle slowed his pace, wondering if he could go back, perhaps stay overnight at the office. He could sleep on the sofa in the reception area. But, no; that was foolish. He couldn't do such a thing. What on earth would people think if they found him there?

Just then, a slim figure bent forward out of an adjacent alley, sniggering. Trendle realised the sound was not snickering laughter, but the figure's feet trailing the black plastic bags that littered the ground.

"Evening," he said; a reflex reaction.

The figure straightened, became upright. It was so thin it might not even be a figure at all. He couldn't make out its features in the gloom. The plastic bags ceased their jittery noise, as if silenced by his presence.

"You haven't seen me." The voice was low, flat, without accent or inflection. The words fell slowly and heavily, like stones in a black river.

"I'm sorry? What was that?"

The dark figure became darker still as it retreated into the mouth of the alley, moving smoothly and silently, as if on castors or pulled by strings. Trendle's vision dimmed and then brightened: a fluke reaction to that stealthy movement in the darkness. When the figure was no longer visible, the order – for that's surely what it was – came again, cold and disembodied. "You haven't seen me."

Trendle hurried past the alleyway, stepping off the kerb and walking on the road, just in case someone lurched out to grab him. Nobody did. He made it to the bus stop unscathed.

The bus was quiet. Only two other passengers rode with him: an old woman wearing iPod headphones and a much younger woman who seemed to be weeping softly as she read a paperback book. The weeper disembarked two stops before Trendle; the old woman remained on the bus when he got off, her head nodding back and forth to whatever tune was playing in her ears.

Trendle walked the few hundred yards from the bus stop in a state of repressed panic, and when he unlocked his front door, stepped inside, then locked it again, he leaned against the wall and tried to stop himself from crying.

What if that mugger from all those years ago had returned to finish him off? Who knew how these people thought? Perhaps he'd even been stalking Trendle ever since the incident, waiting patiently for the right time to make himself known. The police couldn't help – they'd been useless last time. Nobody could help; he was entirely on his own.

He made a late dinner of beans on toast and picked at it without much enthusiasm. Afterwards, he watched a documentary on television, something about a woman who'd pretended to be a survivor of 9/11 when in reality she had not been there at all. Her smug, fat face haunted him as he climbed the stairs to bed, trailing him from the screen to his room. There seemed to be some sort of correlation to her story and the events earlier this evening, but he was unable to understand what it might be.

He slept badly, tossing and turning and mumbling. He woke himself up twice, and each time he thought he saw a far-too-slender figure bending outwards from the wall. He heard a whispered voice: "You haven't seen me." But the voice was only in his mind. He knew that; he was certain of it.

In the morning he felt tired and on edge. His back ached. His scalp itched. He thought he might be coming down with something, so he emailed work and told them he wouldn't be going in for a couple of days.

He spent the day doing nothing. His head was filled with televised images of the World Trade Centre towers toppling, and the repeated phrase he'd heard on his way home last night.

He couldn't go out. Everything outside his front door seemed threatening. People walked by his front window, bent almost double, as if they were carrying heavy burdens. He could not make out their faces; they were slim and dark and frightening.

When night fell, he was unable to move from the living room. The silent television flickered; but no, it was his eyes, his vision fading and re-establishing itself like a cheap nightclub strobe effect. He remembered this happening after the attack. He'd sat on the ground for a long time afterwards, waiting for his vision to return to normal, wondering if something behind his eyes was dislodged by the violence.

Eventually he was too tired to sit up any longer. He reached out and grabbed the remote control, flicked the channel on the television. The image on the screen went to black for a second, and he saw reflected there a figure. It was tall, absurdly thin, and bent forward at the waist, as if caught in the act of emerging from the darkened plasma rectangle.

He heard the words before they were even spoken – if they were spoken at all.

"You haven't seen me."

He felt a slight pressure on his shoulder, as if a hand were resting there. Slowly, he turned his head to look behind him. There was nobody there. Of course there wasn't. He was scaring himself, allowing his imagination to run wild simply because he'd been taken by surprise by a beggar in a back alley.

He turned back to the television screen, at the same time switching off the set with the remote control, which was still in his hand. Just before the screen went dark, he caught sight of an odd image on whatever programme was airing: a static shot of the back of a man's head. The hairstyle looked like Trendle's own, and he'd recognise the shape of the head anywhere.

Trendle stood and turned out the lights. He went

upstairs, feeling stalked but refusing to turn around and acknowledge his weakness. He went to bed without bothering to wash or to clean his teeth. Why bother with such details anyway, when there was no one in his life to benefit from them? He was alone; he had always been alone; the only thing he had to keep him company was his own formless dread.

That night he dreamed of dark alleys, backwards moving figures, and the rear of someone's head rising up from behind his desk at work. He woke before daylight, sweating and afraid. He couldn't get back to sleep, so he sat up in bed and stared at the bedroom door, praying the handle would not turn.

He went back to work because he could think of nothing else to fill his time. He couldn't sit there all day and watch television, and the thought of being outside for any length of time held little appeal.

That evening he left the office on time. He didn't want to walk by that same alleyway, so he chose a different route – one that took him slightly out of his way but seemed a lot safer. He got on the bus and watched the streets pass by like a film set outside the window. Every face he saw looked sad; each person looked grey and pale and weighed down by unfathomable miseries. He wondered if anyone was happy, or if they all felt like him: hollow, empty, discarded.

He got off the bus a stop early and went into a pub he knew. It was a nice place, quiet: a generic brewery-owned theme bar, with framed football jerseys on the walls and a screen above the long wooden bar that showed non-stop sporting highlights. He drank five pints of a local bitter – much more than he was used to consuming in a single session – without speaking to anyone. When he started feeling dizzy he decided to leave.

On his way out the door, a woman barged out of the toilets and brushed against his arm. He turned, holding the door open with one hand, and said, "Sorry."

The woman stopped. She smiled. "No, my fault. Hang on...don't I know you?"

They'd worked together for five years. He saw her almost every day at the photocopier or in the basement print room. She never spoke to him and not once did he try to instigate a conversation. They were just faces passing in the rooms and corridors of the council offices, going about their business as if separated by a sheet of glass.

"No," he said, feeling small and hopeless. "I don't think so."

She screwed up her eyes and pushed her head forward, as if trying to see through a mist. "No, I'm sure we do. You look very familiar."

He smiled. He held open the door. He wished he could turn away and leave, but politeness held him in place. He'd never been able to end a conversation. He always hung around until the other person got bored and made up an excuse to leave.

"Can I buy you a drink?"

He let the door swing shut and followed her back to the bar, where she ordered two cocktails without even asking him what he wanted. For the first time since he could remember, he felt noticed...someone had acknowledged his presence in the world.

"This'll put hairs on your chest," she said, grinning.

Trendle realised she was slightly drunk. Perhaps that was why she couldn't remember how they knew each other. It was almost certainly the reason she'd felt sorry enough for him to offer him a drink.

"I'm celebrating my divorce," she said, after they'd exhausted what little small talk Trendle was capable of. "I lost my friends up the road about half an hour ago…didn't want to go home, so decided to stay. I'm glad we bumped into each other. It saves me from drinking alone."

Trendle raised his glass, took a long swallow of something sickly-sweet. "Me, too," he said. And he really meant it. He was sick and tired of being on his own. Maybe this was what he needed to kick-start the rest of his life – a night spent talking to someone, focusing on things other than himself and having a similar type of attention turned upon him, even if it was out of drunken pity. Other people did it, so why not he? Wasn't he just the same as everyone else?

After a while she moved and sat next to him, her warm thigh touching his leg. She smiled a lot, put her hand on his knee, giggled whenever he said something he didn't think was all that funny.

Trendle realised what she was doing, and he welcomed her advances. She was lonely, drunk, in need of affection and companionship. Just like he was.

"I don't live far from here," he said, recalling a line he'd once heard in a film. "We could go back there. For coffee?"

She took her hand away from his knee. Her face seemed to fall inwards, deflated.

Right then, he knew he'd crossed some kind of line.

"What kind of woman do you think I am?" She was swaying slightly in the chair. She slammed the palm of her hand against the table top.

"I'm sorry…I…"

"You what? You thought you were onto a winner, eh? Thought I'd go back to yours and jump your bones?"

"No…there's been a mistake. I'm not very good at this."

"You can say that again, mate." She stood, moved unsteadily away from the table. "If I hadn't bought this myself, I'd throw it in your face." She brandished her glass, threw back her head in a theatrical manner, and stalked away across the room to the end of the bar, where she started talking to a group of men who'd been watching her performance.

People were staring. They were noticing him, but not in a way that he desired.

Trendle left without finishing his drink.

Outside, the cold air was like a slap in the face. What had he been thinking? He'd misread the situation completely, just as he always did. He always seemed out of step with everyone else; it was as if they were working to a set of rules he hadn't been allowed to see.

He hoped the woman wouldn't recognise him at work tomorrow. He'd have to hide from her, making sure he sent someone else to do the photocopying or collect the printed reports from downstairs. He couldn't risk the shame; he didn't want to confront her when she was sober. God, what if she told everyone about him and when he arrived in the morning they all laughed, or, worse still, just stared at him, smiling at their shared joke?

When would he ever learn? He wasn't like everyone else. He was different…he was socially defective. That's why he'd been mugged, and why the mugger had come back for more. His inadequacies marked him out like a scar or a birthmark. He would always be a victim. He was born to be stepped on.

Inside his house, he went to the kitchen and made a cup of tea. He drank it sitting at the dining table, with the radio playing in the background. He refused to wipe the tears from his eyes because to do so would be to admit he was crying. When his mother was alive, she always taught him that real men never cried.

Perhaps he should quit his job? That way, there'd be no fear of ever seeing that woman again? What was her name, anyway? She'd not offered it this evening, and he hadn't even thought to ask. He could barely think ill of her for not being aware of how they knew each other when he couldn't even remember her name.

Christ, he was pathetic. He saw the woman every day and he didn't even know what she was called.

He finished his tea, locked up the house, and climbed the stairs. Tonight he decided he'd brush his teeth before turning in. His mouth tasted bitter; his teeth were coated with something greasy and unpleasant. His thoughts began to turn: if one woman could approach him, maybe others would, too. It gave him a reason to take care of himself. Why shouldn't he try to take something positive from the disastrous encounter?

The first floor landing seemed cold. He might have to turn the heating on before long. The season was changing. Everything was moving on. No matter how hard he might wish otherwise, nothing ever stayed the same.

He left the lights off because he knew his way by instinct. He'd lived here by himself for a long time, and before that he'd inhabited the space with his mother, who always instilled in him a belief that nowhere was ever as safe as your own home. There were times when he questioned that theory, but not many of them. Often he thought what she really meant was the dangers here were simply more manageable than the ones he might find elsewhere.

His feet were silent as he walked. It seemed odd they should not make a sound, but not odd enough to make him stop and think about the reasons why. It was an old house. The acoustics were weird. His mother had always crept about soundlessly, like a ghost.

The bathroom light flickered when he pulled the chord. He turned and approached the mirror and at first he failed to understand what was wrong with his reflection in the glass. Then, as the light bulb settled, he realised exactly what he was seeing. In the mirror, instead of his own face he was looking at the back of someone's head. *His* head…he recognised the hair colour, the way it turned upwards at his collar, the tiny bald patch at the crown. It was a disconcerting impression, as if he'd sneaked up behind himself. He recalled the same image from the television a few nights ago, and wondered if he'd perhaps glimpsed the future on the screen.

The light flickered again. The filament clicked like an insect rubbing its legs together. He wasn't afraid. Surely there was nothing to fear here, in his home, in his body, in his familiar image.

The figure in the mirror slowly began to turn.

A thin hand pressed down onto his shoulder, the long fingers clutching, holding him in place.

The head in the mirror completed its turn, the skin of the neck corkscrewing because the body remained facing the other way, as if held there by some unnatural force.

When the face came into view, he saw his own features, but altered. The smiling mouth was too wide for the narrow skull. The eyes were dark and spaced too far apart, located almost on the sides of the head. The nose was flat and boorish, the nostrils flared. The cheekbones were much more prominent than his.

The flat, broad lips opened to reveal far too many rows of thin, serrated teeth, which ground together silently.

The voice, when it came, sounded as if it were coming from behind him, despite the mouth in the mirror moving to form the words. It sounded nothing like his voice, the one he'd known his entire life. It was much more assertive, for a start. So much more commanding than anything he could summon. It was the same voice he'd heard when he was mugged, the same one that had spoken to him from the mouth of that alley the other night.

"You haven't seen me. I was never here."

He opened his mouth but was unable to speak. He wanted desperately to agree with this thing so it would leave him alone, but the muscles in his throat refused to work. He didn't want this, not any of it. He had never wanted anything like this.

Reality cracked open and strange feelings leaked out; he thought about concepts that had never before crossed his mind. This thing – this reformed mirror image – was what had been waiting for him all along beneath the brittle façade of his persona: something he could not acknowledge, a creature he wasn't allowed to admit he'd ever seen, despite the fact that it had been hiding inside him since the day he was born.

The bathroom light flickered one more time before going out. Glass shattered and showered the floor with lethal fragments. He closed his eyes. "I haven't seen you," he whispered.

Something that smelled like himself loomed towards him in the darkness, and Trendle prayed it would take him quickly and quietly, and not cause too much pain as it became him.

The Grotto

"Aunty Nancy's locked herself in the toilet again." Dad stood in the doorway, his hand gripping the doorframe, the knuckles turning white. "You'd better sort her out." He walked into the room and sat down on the end of the sofa, avoiding all contact with Mum.

"Oh, Christ..." Mum stood and started to leave the room. "Not this again."

Billy looked at Dad; Dad smiled, but it was a tired expression, one that looked almost defeated.

"It's okay," said Dad. "She'll be fine. She's just...getting old."

Billy turned his attention back to the television and watched a parade of costumed children singing as they crossed a large stage. He wondered, briefly, when Christmas had suddenly become such a chore.

Dad poured himself another whisky and picked up his book – it was an autobiography by some politician Billy had never heard of. Mum had bought it for him, along with the usual socks and underpants and a box of jellied fruit.

"I'm going outside," said Billy, standing and grabbing his coat off the back of the dining chair where he'd left it. "See if anyone's about."

Dad nodded, grunted, but did not look up from his hardback.

Billy stepped out into the hall and stood there for a while, watching Mum.

"Come on, Nancy. Please, let me in. Nobody's angry with you. I just want to see if you're okay." She turned her head to Billy and raised her eyebrows, trying to make light of the situation. But her hard forearms were shaking and her face was pale. Billy remembered last year, when Aunty Nancy had done the same thing, afraid because she'd shit in her knickers.

He walked along the hall and opened the door. The day was growing dark. Winter slush filled the flower beds. Grey scraps of yesterday's snow decorated the lawn. The street was quiet; most people were probably having a snooze after their Christmas dinner, or waiting for the James Bond film to come on.

Billy walked down the path and opened the gate. He looked left along the street, then right. There was no traffic. A hush fell across the estate, and he could pretend he was the only person left in the world. But then the fantasy was broken by the flashing Christmas lights and paper Santas in his neighbours' windows, the muted sounds of someone breaking into a Christmas carol.

He walked along the footpath and stopped outside the gate of Number 10. The garden was overgrown. There were a lot of items dumped on the grass and up against the house wall – old bicycle frames, a broken bathtub, a chest of drawers, cardboard boxes filled with water-bloated newspapers. Billy didn't know who lived there, but they were messy. He couldn't remember who used to live there before the new people moved in, either, but he did know the grotto had always been there.

He stared at it now, feeling the familiar sense of creeping dread. Somebody had wrapped a string of tatty tinsel around the entrance, and a small plaster Santa Claus with a cracked face lay face-up on the ground, as if he'd taken a drunken tumble.

The grotto was made out of old stone slabs with a slate

roof. Whoever built it had constructed uprights and then set a stone lintel across the top to form an entrance. It was roughly two-feet high and six-feet long. It looked more than a little like a megalithic dolmen Billy had once seen, and become briefly obsessed with, in a history book. He had been terrified of the grotto for as long as he could remember. Something about the way he could never see more than half a foot inside the entrance, no matter how bright the daylight, unnerved him.

The house looked empty. There were no lights on. The decorations at the window were old and sagging. Billy pushed open the gate and walked up the cracked concrete path, stopping at a point adjacent to the grotto. Sometimes he liked to test himself. He'd walk to this point, then inch closer and closer towards the entrance, waiting to see how long it would take him to get too scared and run away.

Scabs of snow adhered to the walls and the roof slates. Inside, the darkness seemed to move like hundreds of beetles crawling across a wall. He blinked and the movement stopped. He took another step closer and then the darkness began to twitch again. There was something in there, but he had no idea what it might be.

"No way," he said, then turned his back on the grotto, walked back down the path, shut the gate, and headed home.

Back inside, Aunty Nancy had been coaxed from the bathroom. She was sitting in an armchair gripping a glass of sherry as if it were some kind of life-preserver. She watched the television, nodding her head occasionally. She laughed, a harsh barking sound, and then fell silent again.

Dad was still reading his book. Mum was fussing around the dining table, moving things, putting away the posh cutlery and pouring peanuts into bowls.

"I'm going upstairs," said Billy. Nobody answered.

He played with his new action figures for a while, and then counted his Christmas money. Fifty pounds, enough to get that new Xbox game he'd been eyeing up. His parents had bought him a couple of games, but neither of them was the one he'd wanted.

He tried to read a comic but the colours bled between the panels, and he realised he was tired. Lying down on the bed, he closed his eyes, but all he could see behind the lids was the grotto. In the dream, he was standing closer to it than ever before, reaching out, reaching inside the little entrance. He felt a cold breeze on his hand and smelled a faint aroma of rotting meat. He pulled back his hand, panicked, and saw that it had been replaced by a large, furred claw...

He woke up sweating and breathing heavily; his heart was pumping hard and fast. Gripping the duvet, he waited for the anxiety to pass. He had not experienced an attack in months. Everyone told him how well he was doing now he'd come off the medication.

He managed to calm himself down and sat up on the bed, then looked out of the window. It was dark outside. The streetlights had come on. His watch showed it was 5 p.m. Not late at all.

He stood and crossed to the window. Out on the street, his friend Tony was sitting on the wall outside his house playing on his new Nintendo DS. Billy made a fist and banged on the window. It took Tony a long time to look up, but when he did he waved, motioning for Billy to come out and join him.

Billy went downstairs and opened the door. Glancing

back along the hallway, he watched the play of television light around the living room door, and heard muttered voices. He didn't want to go in there.

"I'm going out," he called. Then he said it again, louder this time.

Nobody answered.

He went outside and crossed the road, sat down on the wall next to Tony.

"How's it going?"

Tony shrugged. He set down his DS on the wall next to him. "Okay, I guess. My folks are arguing again."

"You're lucky," said Billy. "I wish mine would argue. They just sit around all day in a strop with each other."

"Did you get any good stuff?"

"I did okay. I see you got the DS."

"Yeah. It's cool. I only got a couple of games, but I got some money so I can buy some myself."

Billy nodded. "Cool." He looked across the road, at Number 10. The lights were still out. "Have you seen them?"

Tony looked over there, too. "The new people? No, I haven't. Mum says they're feckless."

"What does that mean?"

"Dunno...but Dad called them spongers, and said they don't work. Just claim the dole and sit around on their arses all day, smoking cigs."

"They never seem to be in...so they couldn't be sitting around on their arses."

"Unless they always do it with the lights off."

"Do 'it?'" Billy sniggered. "Do your folks do 'it' with the lights off?"

"Oh, piss off. You know what I mean." Tony elbowed

him in the ribs, but it didn't hurt. He enjoyed the human contact.

"Tony!"

"That's Mum." He shut the cover of his games console and stared at it.

"Get in here! Turkey sarnies are ready!"

"I bloody hate turkey sarnies. He hopped off the wall and walked along his path, then slammed the door when he went inside.

Billy sat there for a moment or two more, looking over at Number 10. He could see the dim outline of the grotto, and something made him want to look inside. But he was afraid; he was always afraid. He was afraid of everything. He walked across the road, opened the door, and started to climb the stairs to his room. "I'm home," he said, but all he heard by way of reply was the television.

He woke up in the night desperate to pee. Straining to keep it in, he left his room and padded down the stairs to the bathroom, and then urinated in the toilet. When he was done he went back upstairs, but he didn't go straight to his room. Instead, he walked across to the spare room, where Aunty Nancy was staying. He listened at the door; he could hear her loud snoring. Carefully, he pushed open the door and went inside the room. She was a vague hump under the bed sheets. He walked to the side of the bed and stared down at her. The side of her face and a few grey wisps of hair were visible against the pillow.

"Bitch," he whispered. "Fucking bitch." He clenched his hand into a fist, raised it, and then let it fall. He stopped it about an inch away from her old, weathered face. "Easy," he said. "It would be so easy."

Suddenly, he became aware of another presence. He

turned and faced the door. Dad was standing there, framed in the doorway, in his vest and pyjama bottoms. Billy said nothing; he just waited. Dad did not move for what seemed like a long time, and then, finally, he turned away and went back to his and Mum's room. When he heard the door gently close, Billy left the spare room and went back to bed.

#

Boxing Day. More grey skies. More wet sleet in the gutters. They were driving Aunty Nancy back to her sheltered housing, where they were going to meet Mum's brother, Uncle Pete.

"He should take his turn," said Dad, fiddling with the radio, trying to improve the signal as he drove. "It's always us. Every year, it's us."

"He's busy," said Mum.

Dad did not reply.

Tell her, thought Billy. *Shout at her… Make her jump. Shock her into life!*

But Dad did not say another word until they reached the row of squat little bungalows on the outskirts of town.

Uncle Pete wasn't there. They got Aunty Nancy inside and waited for an hour, but he didn't show. Mum received a text message when they were halfway home. She wouldn't tell Dad what it said, just repeated the mantra: "He's busy."

Billy spent the rest of the day in his room. Tony was out somewhere with his parents. Their car didn't drive back along the street and park outside their house until after 7 p.m. Billy watched from his bedroom window as Tony's mum and dad got out of the car, shouting at each other. He couldn't hear what they were saying, but it looked bad. Tony slunk off the back seat and out onto the footpath. He glanced up at Billy's bedroom, shrugged, and followed his bickering parents inside.

That evening he watched television with Mum and Dad. It was an old comedy show, Morecombe and Wise. Dad had loved them as a child. It was tradition, he said. They were forced to watch it.

Dad laughed too loudly at all the bad jokes and Mum just sat there with her arms crossed, uncrossing them occasionally to reach for a chocolate from the box she kept at her feet or to take a sip of wine from the big glass on the coffee table.

Billy couldn't see what was meant to be funny. It was just two old men sleeping in the same bed, and making breakfast together while some stupid music played. He did not understand. None of it made any sense.

He closed his eyes and thought about the grotto. How the darkness inside beckoned to him, and the old stone walls would keep him warm.

"I'm going out," he said, standing.

"Don't be out late." Mum's voice was slurred; the first bottle of wine was empty and she'd opened another.

Dad laughed again, his shoulders shaking. He looked desperate.

Billy went outside and walked over to Tony's house. He stood at the gate and listened to the wordless yelling coming from inside. Shadows moved back and forth across the front window. He heard the sound of breaking glass.

He crossed the road and entered the garden of Number 10. He walked right up to the grotto and stood there, daring it to do something. The stone walls remained upright; the slate roof did not fall in. Darkness swirled inside the entrance.

"What's in there?" He moved closer, bending down to look inside.

He got down on his knees and stuck his head near the entrance. This was the closest he'd ever been to the grotto, and he felt excited and afraid. He realised he had an erection. "Come on…what are you hiding?" He could see nothing, just the shifting blackness, as if a river of night were churning inside the grotto. He felt a chill breeze on his cheek.

He raised his hand, opened his fingers, and reached inside.

Something grabbed hold of his hand, squeezing, tugging gently, trying to pull him inside. He was so afraid that he could not make a sound. His feet drummed against the ground. His other hand grabbed the side of the grotto, bracing his body so it would not be dragged forward.

He pulled.

It pulled back.

Billy was stuck there, locked in a tug-o-war with whatever was trying to pull him inside the grotto. He opened his mouth to scream but was so out of breath only a small, sad sound escaped his lips. He gave one last mighty tug, and his hand came free. He fell backwards, went sprawling on the ground. Moving quickly across the ground on his backside, he made it to the path. Then he stood, turned, and ran. He didn't stop running until he reached his own front door. He dragged it open, slammed it shut, and slid home the bolts.

Billy stood with his back against the door, panting,

gasping, trying to catch his breath. What had just happened? What was that, in the grotto, and why had it tried to drag him into its lair?

He went into the living room and looked at his parents. Mum was stuffing her face with chocolates; Dad was asleep in front of the television.

"Night, love," said his mother. She did not glance in his direction. She sounded drunk.

He turned away, left the room, and slowly climbed the stairs to his bed.

He tried to sleep, but every sound he heard put him on edge. He heard Mum climbing the stairs, using the toilet, weeping behind the bathroom door. Dad followed her upstairs a couple of hours after she'd gone to bed. He heard the creaking of the bed springs, his father farting as he settled in for the night.

Who were these people? Had they ever been happy?

He got out of bed and looked out of the window. From where he was, the angle was all wrong to see the garden of Number 10, but he could see along the edge of the wall forming the boundary to the property. There was a cat sitting on the wall... Or was it a dog? Or maybe an urban fox. Whatever the thing was, it was big, and it started to creep along the top of the wall towards his house, as if it had been waiting there for him to notice. The more he watched, the more convinced he became it was not a cat or a dog or a fox. It was too large, with too many thin, angled legs, and moved much too slowly and awkwardly to be any of those sure-footed animals.

More than anything, it looked like a spider: a huge, grubby, crippled spider moving along the top of the wall.

Billy closed his eyes. When he opened them again the

thing was still there. He closed them again…opened them. This time it was gone. He'd imagined the whole thing. He went back to bed, but was still unable to sleep. He was scared that if he did, something might come into his room, crawl across the floor, and climb up onto his bed.

#

It had snowed overnight.

Billy went downstairs and opened the front door, looking out at the fresh blanket of whiteness. Parked cars were transformed into silken white humps in the road; the roofs of the houses were piled with the stuff. He smiled, staring at its purity. Then he saw the marks. Small indentations, as if someone had used the end of a stick or a pole to poke a track along the garden path from the gate to the front door.

It's real, he thought. *It was here. It came right up to the door.*

"Breakfast," said Mum, behind him. He could smell burning bacon; the frying pan sizzled like a bad radio reception.

They were just starting on their breakfast when the phone rang.

"What?" said Mum, obviously shaken by whatever she was being told. "Now? Okay…don't worry. We'll go over there."

She hung up the phone.

"That was Pete."

Dad looked up from his plate. "What is it this time?"

Mum would not look him in the eye as she spoke. She looked everywhere but at Dad's face: the walls, the sink, the dining table. "It's Aunty Nancy. She's ranting and raving, throwing things, breaking things. Her next-door neighbour called Pete. But Pete's busy. We have to go."

"Jesus," said Dad, rising from his chair.

"He's busy." Mum at last looked directly into Dad's face. Her eyes were blazing.

By the time they reached the sheltered housing she was calmer. There was no noise coming from inside. The old neighbour man was standing on his lawn, watching as Mum opened the door with her spare key and they trooped inside. Aunty Nancy was sitting on the ugly patterned carpet in the middle of the room. Her skirt was hitched up over her flabby knees.

"Aunty Nancy? It's us. Are you okay?"

She did not respond. She just sat there, staring at the wall.

Dad called an ambulance and they took her away. Billy watched as she was helped into the back of the vehicle, mute and with no fight left in her. She looked like a bag of bones, all soft and floppy and defeated.

I never want to be like that.

He glanced at Mum and Dad, ashamed of his thoughts. They looked the same, as if all the life was drained out of them. He could not remember the last time he'd seen them hold hands, or share a tender kiss. They never even touched each other.

After the hospital, they went back home. It was early evening; they'd been out all day. Billy stared up at the sky, at the stars as they were coming out, at the flat, bright crescent of the moon.

He waited up as late as he could, hoping Mum and Dad would retire to bed before him. But they didn't; they sat up, not speaking to each other, losing themselves in the television. So Billy went slowly to his room, wondering when this would all come to an end.

They couldn't go on like this. None of them. It had to be stopped. He knew that now… He had no choice.

When the house went quiet, and he no longer heard the creaking of bed springs in his parents' room, he got up and went outside. He walked slowly but purposefully down the street. He'd taken the rest of the Christmas turkey out of the fridge; cold cuts wrapped in foil. He hoped whatever was in the grotto was hungry. He hoped it liked meat.

The house lights were on at Number 10, but this did not deter him. In a funny way, it seemed like encouragement; the new people were giving him a sign. He went into the garden and knelt down in front of the grotto. It looked even more decrepit than the last time. Some of the roof slates were loose. The walls were bowed. He opened the foil package and took out the scraps of turkey, then laid them out on the ground outside the grotto. He stood, walked backwards to the gate, and waited.

"I'm ready. I'm ready for you now."

The darkness just inside the grotto's entrance began to twitch, and then it began to boil. He looked away just as a small, dark shape started to inch forward, moving painstakingly over the threshold.

He walked slowly along the street, making sure it would follow. He could hear pinprick feet crunching in the brittle snow behind him. He did not want to turn around and look. If he did, it might vanish. Or, even worse, it might prove to be real.

This can't go on, he thought again. *This is where it ends.*

He walked though his garden gate, approached the front door and opened it. Then he stepped to the side and turned his face away. From the edge of his vision, he saw something squat and creased with too many legs shuffle over the doorstep and go inside.

Whatever the thing was, it was made of discarded condoms and crisp packets, soggy leaves, broken twigs, crushed and rusted beer cans and those little plastic tie-bags people fill with dog shit when they're out walking the family pet; it was held together with glue concocted from love and hate and resentment and all the complex emotions growing like mould in between. Its legs were pipe cleaners and lolly sticks. It smelled of dusty decay. It had the small white face of a shattered Plaster of Paris Santa Claus.

Billy's need had somehow summoned this mix-and-match creature, this lucky-dip monstrosity, bringing it forth into the wider world outside the grotto.

He closed the door and sat down on the step, placing one foot behind the opposite ankle. It started to snow. A car moved slowly and quietly along the road past the house. Somewhere on the estate, a dog barked. Billy shivered.

"Happy Christmas," he said, closing his eyes and clenching his fists.

Then he waited for the screaming to start.

Hungry Love

Stan wasn't looking for love. Oh no, not this time. In fact, after the bitter and painful ending to his previous relationship, it was the last thing on his agenda. But he knew, as everyone knows, that love – or, as in this case, a *lust* that holds the promise of turning into love – often finds you when you're least interested in encountering that particular emotion, or even when you're hiding from it.

Especially when you're hiding from it.

Sometimes these things just creep into your life when you're not looking, and despite anything you might do to prevent it, they decide to set up camp and stay.

#

"Thanks for that, Ted." Stan felt like he was speaking just for the sake of it, to force some kind of connection between them. "I, er...enjoyed what you had to say."

The other man smiled. He was putting his laptop back in its case and struggling with the cable as he tried to tuck it down the side of the machine. "Thanks. I often feel like people only attend these lunchtime seminars for the free sandwiches." He smiled again. He was beautiful: a long narrow face, high cheekbones, thick hair.

Beautiful.

"Well, they *were* good...especially those ones with the salmon and cucumber, and the crusts cut off."

Ted shook his head, but he was grinning. "I know, I know...you people only want me for my catering."

"Oh, I want more than that." The words were out there

before Stan had the chance to stop them. He closed his mouth, much too late to repair any damage that might have been caused. Then, feeling scared, he waited. The clock on the meeting-room wall ticked too loudly. The traffic outside was deafening. The moment stretched, becoming a lifetime.

Ted glanced up, his long, thin fingers now zipping shut the laptop case. Stan imagined them unzipping his trousers. He looked to the window, unable to hold the other man's gaze. The low trees outside the office trembled in a breeze.

"Oh," said Ted. All the other sounds died away, making room for his voice.

"Sorry." Stan began to turn away. He'd made a mistake.

"Don't be." Ted smiled again. His teeth were too white to be natural: he must've spent a fortune on dental work. "I'm flattered. Really, I am."

"But?" Stan hovered by the table, ready to bolt. He stared hard at Ted's features, looking for even the slightest hint of mockery but detecting none.

"What do you mean?"

"Oh, there's always a 'but.'"

Ted shook his head. "Not this time, mate." Now his smile could only be described as lascivious. "Unless you mean *my* gorgeous lily-white butt…"

#

They didn't even bother to go out for a drink and get to know each other first. There was no shared dessert after a romantic meal, no holding hands across a restaurant table, not even a smattering of Dutch courage imbibed in a nearby bar. Stan took his new lover straight back to his place immediately after work, and they fucked first on the stairs, then on the upstairs landing, and finally in the bed.

Ted's body was smooth and tanned – his butt was far from being lily-white; in fact it was a rather fetching nut-brown, which bespoke either of naked sunbed sessions or prolonged spells on nudist beaches. His spit tasted of vanilla and his spunk was very salty. He liked to hum Beatles songs under his breath when he was being fellated, and his palms were dry and rough, like a cat's tongue.

Stan liked all of these things. He liked them and he wanted to experience them more fully, and countless times in a row. As often as possible, in fact.

"How the hell did that happen?" They were lying on their backs on the bed, holding hands. Clutching, really, rather than holding. Or perhaps *clasping* was a better word. They were both breathing deeply, shattered after the monumental bout of lovemaking.

"I'm…not sure." Stan was struggling for breath. He'd not done this for a long time – brought a virtual stranger back home for sex. It reminded him of his old habits, when his life had been a lot messier and he enjoyed placing himself in situations of controlled danger. Things had been more complicated back then, and he didn't miss that way of life one little bit. He liked things safer these days; he preferred to be in control.

"I'm glad it did happen, though," said Ted, turning his face towards Stan's on the crumpled pillows. "*Really* glad, to be honest." His smile was small but genuine.

"Thank fuck for that," said Stan, still breathless.

They both laughed at that; oh, how they laughed. Like loons.

The two men began to see each other, off and on, over the next few weeks. Soon they were inseparable, like a couple of teenagers experiencing these emotions for the first time. Stan felt himself falling; he liked Ted a lot, and was certain that liking would soon become loving. He knew the signs; he'd been through it all before, at least twice in his life. This was going to be a major relationship: one of those you never forget, even if they end badly. This, he knew, would be memorable.

They spent a lot of time together. Doing things. Being a couple. They went to the park, walked hand-in-hand through the streets, window shopped for clothes they couldn't afford in expensive stores. All the things partners were meant to do – and wasn't that the thing they'd become, a partnership?

They shared a love of old films, black and white classics. The funnies were the best. Stan liked the Marx Brothers, and Ted said he liked them, too. So they sat up late, drinking wine and eating popcorn and watching Stan's worn VHS copies of *Duck Soup*, *A Day at the Races*, and *A Night at the Opera*. Stan thought Ted might be lying about his love of the Marx Brothers, but he didn't say anything about his doubts. He knew the sketches by heart, but Ted laughed as if he were seeing them for the first time. But people did that, didn't they? They pretended to like something that another person liked, just to forge a bond, to hurry along the natural process.

It wasn't a big deal. And Ted lapped up the antics of Groucho, Harpo, Chico, and that other one – the one whose name hardly anybody, even Stan, could ever remember.

In exchange, Ted introduced Stan to the Universal

horror films. *Dracula. Frankenstein. The Wolfman.* Stan had always been too afraid to watch horror films – even silly, dated ones like these – but Ted held his hand and didn't laugh when he jumped in shock at all the right moments. Even when he faked it, just to get a cuddle.

They traded their interests like this, swapping likes, giving each other small gifts of films, music and art. Enjoying the fact that the other also enjoyed (or pretended to, anyway) whatever it was they were being shown. Stan started to suspect Ted might be The One. That fabled lover everyone wanted to meet, but few actually did. He started to imagine the two of them growing old together, maybe adopting a kid, getting married in a hot air balloon. All the things he'd told his friends that he never wanted but secretly did, because he felt they would make his life more complete, like a proper life rather than some strange faded copy he'd picked up in a second-hand shop.

He soon realised he was probably in love.

One night, as they sat in Stan's front room drinking Muscat after a nice pasta dinner, they had The Conversation: the one that always comes along, sooner or later, if things start to move beyond Casual and into the territory of Serious.

"How do you feel…" said Stan, putting down his glass on the table, "about this? About *us*?" He pushed the glass around, causing the wine to slop against the side of the glass. He couldn't look up, into Ted's eyes, just in case he'd misjudged things.

"I knew this was coming," said Ted, before taking another sip of his drink. "I could feel it brewing…like a storm. I suppose it was always just a matter of time."

Stan closed his eyes. *Shit.* He'd fudged it; the man

didn't feel the same way about him, and he'd already put his cards on the table. Right next to the expensive wine glass he was in danger of tipping over.

"There are things you don't know about me. They're not nice things."

Stan kept his eyes shut. "Let me guess...you're a government spy, which means you're not allowed to form lasting relationships? Or you suffer from a rare blood disease and only have a few weeks left to live? I've heard them all before, love. I've even used a few of them myself."

Ted surprised him by reaching out and grabbing his hand. Those long, artistic fingers...they moved as if they had a life of their own, beyond the will of their owner.

"No," said Ted. "This isn't the preamble to me making some big excuse to get rid of you. I know how you feel – it's obvious. You're rubbish at hiding your feelings."

Stan opened his eyes, but he didn't look up. He kept staring at the glass. It was very thin, elegant. A nice glass. He'd always enjoyed quality things.

Ted continued: "And if I let myself, I know I could feel the same way about you."

The air hummed; tension bounced off the objects in the room: the leather sofas, the television, the framed posters and prints on the walls. The window glass seemed to vibrate.

"If you *let* yourself?" It still sounded, to Stan, like some kind of excuse.

"There's something wrong with me, Stan...I'm *different*. I'm not made like everybody else."

"Oh, come off it," said Stan, snatching back his hand. The glass tipped over but he made no move to pick it up.

220

"Just go. Get out, if that's what you want. I won't make a fuss. You don't have to make up some kind of story."

"No, that's not what I want. What I want is to stay here, with you, and have you take me to bed. I want us to be together."

Finally, and with great difficulty, Stan looked up. Ted's thin face was ashen; his tan had faded. His cheeks looked sunken and his eyes had dark smudges around them. Strain had drawn a sketch of his features, and the drawing slowly faded as Stan sat there and watched.

"I'm serious," said Ted. And Stan knew he was telling the truth.

"Okay," he said. He picked up the glass and placed it back on the table in its upright position. The wine had spilled and drained into the plaid tablecloth, so he refilled it with more. He made no move to refill Ted's glass, and he didn't bother wiping up the mess.

"I have so much love inside me...but that love is, well, it's strange."

Stan almost laughed. "What the fuck is that supposed to mean? Jesus, you sound like a cliché, a big queer cliché." Suddenly he wanted to hurt the other man, even more than he wanted to hurt himself.

"No, really. I am filled with love. But it's a dangerous love. A hungry love."

Stan smiled, but it was without humour. "Spare me the crappy song lyrics..."

"That," said Ted, his lips barely moving at all, "is exactly what I'm trying to do. Spare you. At first I had you pegged as just another victim, but now things are different. Everything's changed."

"Bullshit. You're just trying to fob me off, to put me off

you. There's no need for that. You don't have to create some shitty little reason to disguise that you have no feelings for me, that I was just a fuck-buddy. I'll be fine. I'll survive. I always do." He knew that he had also lapsed into cliché, but he couldn't help it: he was doing it on purpose, as if by using overly familiar, melodramatic language he might distance himself from the situation.

"Oh, I have feelings for you," said Ted. He looked sad, as if he was experiencing regret. "I have so much love for you it's practically bursting to get out…" he began to unbutton his shirt. "Here, let me show you."

"One last fuck for the road, eh?" Stan's bitterness tasted bad. It filled his mouth like bile. "Okay, obviously I have no self-respect. Let's go for it."

Slowly, and still with his face reflecting so much sadness, Ted shook his head and continued to open his shirt. He bared his chest, and then took off the garment, casting it aside. The skin below his clavicle was churning, writhing, as if hundreds of maggots were crawling inside his chest. Small ridges and rises; tiny whorls and tracks. It looked like something was inside him, and it was desperate to get out.

"It isn't a metaphor. This is it…this is my *love*."

Stan opened his mouth but no words came out.

Ted used his long, thin fingers to peel back the skin just beneath his ribcage. He pulled it up and over, like another piece of clothing – a T-shirt, or a vest – and kept on pulling until he exposed the layers of dry, withered tissue beneath.

"No," said Stan, at last able to summon a word, even if it was just a small one, and meaningless. "No," he said again, stuck on that single negative declaration.

Ted pressed his fingertips against the middle of his ribcage and pulled the two halves aside like a set of doors. Whatever it was he kept there – his *love*, as Ted called it – responded by swelling and surging out of the gap. It looked like a cluster of jellyfish, all clumped together but with a lot of stunted arms and legs and half-formed mouths. Each of those tiny, lipless openings was rimmed with a circular set of pointed teeth, and the teeth rotated like the blades of a circular saw.

"What the fuck...?" Stan couldn't move. He tried, but he was unable. His body had severed all communications with his brain.

"It's my love...my hungry, hungry love. I try to keep it fed, but I'm not enough. Never enough. It always wants more."

Then, surprising himself, Stan reached out and began to stroke the gelid mass. It was soft and smooth, and slightly cold to the touch, like window putty. The thing responded to his gentle caress, twisting and wrapping part of itself around his hand. If it were a cat, it would have been purring.

"It likes you." Ted reached out and brushed his hand against Stan's cheek. "It likes you as much as I do."

Stan was no longer afraid. It was as if the thing in Ted's chest had taken away his fear, absorbing it and transforming the negative emotion into something much more useful. "How long has it been there, inside you?"

"Always," said Ted. "I was born this way. Filled with hungry love...and usually, in situations like this, it only wants to satisfy that hunger. I groom potential lovers, see them for a while – until they start to love me. Then *my* love devours theirs, turning it into sustenance."

"So why isn't it devouring me," said Stan, feeling high and floaty, as if this were some kind of lucid dream. "I mean, at first, when I saw the thing, I thought that's what it wanted. To eat me. To use me up. But it didn't. All it did was take my fear. Why did it do that?" He pulled his hand away, regretting it instantly. He wanted to keep stroking the thing, feeling its tender, undulating mass under his fingers.

"I don't know," said Ted. "This has never happened before. I told you I had feelings for you…maybe that's why. Because my feelings are real. Or maybe it's getting lonely, and thinks you might be a friend." He closed up his chest and reached for his shirt.

"No," said Stan, pressing his hand against Ted's chest. "Don't." He raised his other hand and began to massage Ted's ribcage. Ted closed his eyes. His lips began to move; he was humming a Beatles song. Penny Lane. One of his favourites.

The ribcage tensed, and then relaxed as Stan fondled it. He felt the thing in Ted's chest reaching out to him, straining to make contact. "I love you," he said, and for the first time he realised he was not talking to Ted; in fact he never had been, all this time.

He was speaking to the *thing* inside Ted.

"I love you, too," said Ted. Then he resumed humming his tune.

Love.

You.

This time Stan only mouthed the words; he didn't want to hear any kind of reply, not from Ted. He wanted to feel it, to experience it by touch alone. The thing in Ted's chest fluttered. It loved him back. Ted's love loved him in return.

They went to bed. Stan was distracted, but he made sure Ted was fully satisfied before falling asleep. As Ted snored softly at his side, flat on his back with one arm raised above his head as if to ward off invisible sunshine, he pulled down the bedclothes, exposing Ted's naked torso.

He'd felt it shifting as they fucked. Kneeling behind Ted, deep inside him past the rim, he had reached around and stroked the other man's chest, feeling around, trying to connect with the thing inside him. Briefly, he'd felt a soft fluttering movement, like huge wings twitching, and then it was gone. When he came, he imagined his ejaculate squirting up inside Ted's rectum, tearing out of the ruined tissue and travelling into his stomach, then up into his chest, and coating the creature which lay curled up there, enjoying the distant sensations of sex.

It was a silly fantasy, he knew, but what about this whole situation wasn't silly? In fact, wasn't it actually insane?

He held his hand, palm down, an inch above Ted's sweaty torso. The skin beneath trembled; the thing knew he was there, and what he was doing. Once again, it was struggling to reach him. Ted slept on, unknowing; he didn't even realise Stan was conducting a secret affair with his love. It was almost funny, if you thought about it. Absurd, yes, but also very funny...

"I love you," he said, lowering his head so his lips touched Ted's flesh. I. Love. You. Love."

The thing in Ted's chest fluttered madly, excited.

It gets hungry.

Ted's earlier words returned to him, filling his head.

Hungry.

But what on earth would such a thing eat? He didn't even want to think about the mechanics of consumption, but the subject of what kind of diet it needed tugged at him, not letting him go.

He thought of old women when they saw little babies, and couples so lost in their feelings they uttered gibberish:

I love you so much I could eat you all up.

He flattened his hands on Ted's chest.

I could eat you up...

He slid his fingers into the small indentation at the centre of Ted's ribcage, feeling the seam in his flesh, and pushed the bones slowly apart. Beneath the epidermis, Ted's muscle mass was desiccated; the meat of him was dry and fibrous, like the layers which made up a sheet of corrugated cardboard.

Eat you up...

He opened up Ted's chest and set his eyes upon Ted's love – *his* love. The love they both shared. It was beautiful, soft and white and diaphanous. It seemed to have changed slightly in appearance, as if this new situation was making it thrive. It was puffy, like cotton candy. The similarities to a jellyfish were a thing of the past; now it looked like a big ball of candy floss. But with teeth, sharp circular teeth.

Stan reached inside and cupped Ted's love. He lifted it out and stared at the empty, dusty space it left behind. There was no heart; there were no internal organs in there at all. No blood, either. Over the years Ted's love had slowly used him up, drained him dry, and now he was just a shell, a container for his love: he was a big, bony box filled with love.

And now, once again, his love was hungry.

I could eat you all up...

He pressed the thing against his cheek. It was soft, downy, and so wonderfully cool. *Like ice cream*, he thought, *not candy floss. But like lovely fluffy ice cream.* He rubbed it against his face, kissed it, enjoying its substance. The thing rolled around on his hands, wrapped itself around his forearms. He buried his face in its mass and breathed in its smell: vanilla, and beneath that the suggestion of fresh meat. He felt its sharp little teeth as they grazed against his chin, nibbling: dainty little love bites.

All his life people had told Stan his kind of love was wrong, it was twisted. That it was *mutant*.

Well, he thought, *I guess they were right after all.*

Then, when he was finished luxuriating, almost regretfully he placed the love onto Ted's upturned face. It spread out, like a stain, covering his handsome features. Ted, waking now, began to struggle feebly, but Stan leaned across his body and restrained him, pinning down his arms. This enabled his love to feast, to sate its hunger and fill itself up with Ted, or what little now remained of him on the bed. The parasite was turning on its host, cleaning up the mess before it entered its new home.

When Ted stopped moving Stan got up and crossed the room, opened the door, and took one last look at the resting place of his former lover, the man with the long, thin fingers and who had so much love to give. A small mound of something or other was still visible on the bed. Soon there'd be nothing left to see – nothing but his love. The sounds it made were muffled, but unpleasant. Small tearing sounds; tiny sucking noises.

Stan loved his love, but its eating habits turned his

stomach.

He left the room and closed the door behind him, cutting off the busy little sounds of feeding.

\#

The man walked into the bar and sat down on a stool. It wasn't a gay bar, or even a pick-up joint. Just a drab city-centre drinking den, quiet and half-empty at this hour of the day. He ordered a large G&T and listened to the jukebox music while he waited. It never took long. Usually within a couple of minutes someone would be drawn to him, attracted to his love, his hungry, hungry love.

"Hi," said the boy. He was young, pretty, and had one of those pouty little mouths the man had always liked.

"Can I buy you a drink?"

The boy nodded. Sat down. "I'll have a Heineken."

"I'm Stan," said the man, staring at the boy, sizing him up. He would do. Thin, with not much meat on his bones, but his shoulders were broad and hard and he stood quite tall: solidly built for someone so skinny.

"Pete," said the boy, nodding and smiling as the barman set down his beer before moving away to stand and watch the football on the television.

"This your local, then, Pete? Is it your neighbourhood watering-hole?"

"You mean, do I come here often?" Pete smiled. His eyes lit up from the inside. He clearly liked to come across as being a bit cheeky, something of a Jack-the-lad: somebody with a slight edge.

"I suppose I do mean that, yes." The man smiled back, but it was empty, lacking any genuine warmth or humour:

a painted-on grin.

"So what's your story?" said Pete, rubbing his leg against the man's thigh. "I mean, what brings you here tonight, Stan the Man?"

"Well," said the man, placing his hands flat on the bar. Something stirred dryly in his chest, turning over to get into a more comfortable position. He clenched his hands into fists. "I suppose you could say I'm a man who's in love with love."

He smiled again, this time more realistically.

Pete raised his glass to his lips.

"You're weird," he said. "But I like weird." Then he took a drink.

The jukebox changed its tune: 'This is Not a Love Song.'

After a moment's pause, the man began to laugh.

Alice, Hanging Out at the Skate Park

Then:

She was found early one morning. The sun was just coming up, its golden light basting the horizon like a layer of butter on a roasting chicken. A man was jogging through the park with his dog. I think it was an Irish Setter. He cut down behind the old bowling pavilion, along the narrow, leaf-coated pathway between the damp flower beds, and came out of the trees by the kiddie's play park. He ran past the empty swings and slides and climbing frames, and turned the corner to run alongside the skate park.

He saw her immediately.

She was a small girl; everyone used to call her "dainty." She had such tiny hands and feet. She wore clothes made for someone two or three years younger than her. She was lying vertically down one of the stainless steel skating ramps with a length of nylon washing line wrapped around her throat, her bare feet pointing downward. The other end of the line was tied to a metal tent peg hammered into the ground a few yards away, at the rim of the slope bordering the sunken skate park.

There was a transparent plastic bag over her head. The plastic was pressed so tightly against her skin she looked shrink-wrapped.

She was just eighteen years old.

They never discovered who killed her.

Three months later:

"I wish they'd just take her away."

I stopped beside one of the wooden benches and glanced at my wife, Emma. She was staring at Dead Girl – that's what they all called her now, like a nickname – and I could see the side of her face. Her features were sharp: severe cheekbones, a chiselled nose. Most people thought she was elegant but I just thought she looked vaguely evil, a bit like a wicked witch in a picture book.

"They do," I said. "They do take her away. Every day."

Emma turned towards me. The sun was now positioned behind her head; her hair was wreathed in yellow fire. "But they used to do it four or five times a day. Why did they stop?"

I shrugged. "Don't ask me. Maybe they got sick of wasting their time."

She glanced again at Dead Girl, and slowly shook her head. "What's her name again?"

"Alice," I said, too quickly. "I believe it was Alice."

"Well, I wish she'd fuck off through the looking glass." Emma walked away towards the fence to watch Ben play. He was on the big climbing frame, carefully working his way to the top of the roped pyramid.

I walked up next to her and placed my hand on her thigh. She ignored the gesture. I left my hand where it was, too embarrassed to take it away.

"I hope he doesn't fall," she said.

I examined Alice, in her little taped off resting place on the skating ramp. She was wearing the same clothes as always: a dark blue knee-length hooded coat, black leggings cut off at the shin, and a tight black woollen sweater. Her feet were dirty. She hadn't changed a bit.

Ben finished on the climbing frame and went over to the swings. He clambered into one and started himself off by rocking back and forth, then looked over at us pleadingly. "Dad..." His face was pale. He was a beautiful boy, but fragile. That was why Emma always worried so much about him. She hated to see him taking too many risks.

I walked along beside the waist-height metal fence and opened the gate, moving over to the swings. The play park was busy, full of happy little families enjoying the day. I stood behind Ben and pulled the swing backward, then paused before letting it go. He laughed as I pushed him higher and higher. His legs kicked out at the apex of each arc, and he let out a little squeal of pleasure every time he swept down towards me.

When we were finished Ben wanted an ice cream, so we walked through the gate to get Emma. She was concentrating on the council workmen as they removed Alice's body. They cut the nylon washing line, hauled her onto the rear of a tiny little dumper truck, and then drove off over the concrete skate park. A small crowd was gathering, as usual. Some of them – the younger ones – were laughing. It was no big deal. This happened every day, just another part of park life.

By the time they'd reached the far end of the park, Alice's body was once again at the ramp. Nobody ever saw it reappear; it just did. Even if you watched the space intently, not even blinking, you could never pinpoint the exact moment she returned to the ramp, the nylon line wrapped firmly around her throat, her arms lying stiff at her sides, her face a mashed blur through the plastic bag.

"I hate it," said Emma. She wrapped her arms around her rib cage, holding herself. "It's horrible."

I studied the people as they moved away from Alice's body after the removal; once she was back in place they lost interest and dispersed. A number of the others hadn't even bothered to watch. They were getting used to the event. The newspaper and television reporters didn't even turn up any more, unless it was a slow news day. It was an old story; other, more important stuff was happening: celebrities having affairs, new films being released, riots in European cities.

We walked through the park, watching people playing football, climbing trees, sitting on the grass with sandwiches and flasks of tea. I bought Ben a large cone at the ice cream stall. Emma didn't want anything, and neither did I. We headed towards the exit and the main road. We crossed the road and walked a few hundred yards to our street, and went home.

#

Later that night, when Ben was in bed, I opened a bottle of wine.

"Thanks," said Emma as I poured her a glass. Her hand was like a big albino spider clutching the glass.

I poured myself a drink and sat down next to her on the sofa, pretending not to notice when she moved fractionally away from me. The television was on. Some film was playing – I didn't recognise any of the actors. I sipped my wine, tried not to think about anything.

"You knew her, didn't you?"

I felt like I'd been caught out. It was as if some great

and terrible secret had been revealed, one I hadn't even known. "Who do you mean?"

"Dead Girl. Alice. Whatever she's called... You knew her when she was alive."

I took another sip of my wine, ostensibly to buy some time. I had no idea what I was going to say next.

"Don't bother lying."

I held my breath. "Yes, I knew her."

"Why didn't you tell me?"

"How long have you known?"

She smiled. "I've always known. I've been waiting for you to say something."

I exhaled through stiff lips. My face felt like it was made out of stone. "When they found her like that, I thought the police might come by if they figured out I knew her. I didn't want to get involved."

"How did you meet her?"

I sighed. "She attended a couple of classes, dropped out after a few weeks. She wasn't cut out for creative writing."

"How come the police didn't know about that? Surely her name would be on the college records."

"Night classes are different. We just rent the room from the college. They have no involvement other than that. She turned up to try out the class, didn't enjoy it, and failed to return. It happens all the time. I don't usually ask people to sign on officially until a month or so into the course. It frightens some of them off."

She stared at me with her unnerving, slightly hostile gaze. I knew most men thought her desirable, but these days she left me feeling cold. I couldn't even remember what initially drew me to her, why we had ended up getting married in the first place. Then Ben came along and it didn't matter. None of it mattered any more. We had a child. Everything else was shaped around that one thing. We were already trapped.

"What?" I felt my face turning red. My cheeks were hot.

"Nothing…I'm just checking if you're telling me the truth."

"What, with your X-ray vision?"

"Yes, with my patented X-ray vision." She smiled. "If I thought you were lying to me…well, just don't be. You don't want to know what would happen if you are."

"I'm not lying. I have nothing to lie about."

But I did. I was. I was lying through my teeth.

Before:

I met Alice, as I'd told Emma, through my twice-weekly evening class in creative writing. She came along once, stayed behind after the lesson, and told me I was talking crap. I asked her to explain, and she said she'd tell me everything over a drink in the pub down the road.

I didn't hesitate.

"You're not even a published author," she said, gripping a glass of cider. Her eyes were big and dark. Her face was oval-shaped. She was wearing fingerless gloves; she'd refused to take them off, even indoors. The pub was quiet. It was a week night; the weather was bad; there was a good film on television. Something like that.

"I had a book published several years ago."

"It was eleven years ago," she said. "I Googled you. And it was a book on mountain biking. You're teaching creative writing. How can you justify that when you aren't even qualified?"

I shook my head and smiled. "Okay, you got me. Guilty as charged. Cuff me and read me my rights."

A little over an hour later we were fucking in my car.

I drove to a secluded lane on the outskirts of town and we started necking like teenagers. She grabbed my cock through my trousers. I moaned; the pressure was unbearable, as if my pocket was full of ball bearings. She laughed into my mouth as we kissed. Then she unzipped me and stuck her hand inside my pants.

The car seats didn't recline far enough, so it was awkward, but we managed to locate a rhythm. She straddled me, and as we worked at it I stared over her shoulder at the darkness beyond the windscreen, holding on for dear life. I saw the spindly limbs of autumn trees twitching towards us, small, singular clouds scudding across the dark sky, the lights of an aircraft as it flew overhead. Then I experienced the strange sensation I was looking in at myself looking out. It only lasted a moment, but it was a strange moment, and not at all unpleasant.

As she approached an orgasm, I noticed the thick layer of dust on the dashboard. The car could do with a clean. Finally I let myself go; my own orgasm came seconds before hers did, but I kept on pumping anyway in the hope that she wouldn't lose a grip on it.

Afterwards, she sat in the passenger seat with her head resting on my shoulder. It wasn't a comfortable position, but I didn't want to offend her by moving away. My leg started to itch, just above the knee. I concentrated on not moving. I wanted to see how long I could last before I was forced to scratch.

She lit up a cigarette. I opened the window, scratching

my leg.

"Sorry," she said. But she wasn't. She continued to smoke, blowing it into the car.

"It's okay." I tried not to breathe in the smoke.

I didn't even find her attractive. She wasn't my type at all, and way too young to be messing with. My sleeping with her was nothing but another indication of how bad my marriage was. I didn't want to do it again.

We met the following week, after class. Then it became a regular thing.

After a while she didn't even pretend she was interested in what I had to say. We drove to the same lonely spot, had sex in the same clumsy position, and she smoked the same brand of cigarettes afterwards. I usually experienced that same vaguely out-of-body experience just before I came, but it was never as intense as the first time.

We never spoke once we'd done it. She smoked a couple of cigarettes. I opened the window. Then I drove her home.

One time I didn't turn up for my own class. I wanted to end the thing with Alice but wasn't brave enough to tell her to her face.

Two weeks later she was dead in the skate park.

Now:

When the police came round I was too shocked to say anything.

I let the officers in – there were two of them, a man and a woman – and sat down on the sofa. Emma was out at her yoga class. She wouldn't be home for a couple of hours. I wondered if it was her who'd told the police, or one of her friends. Not that it mattered. I'd always known they'd work it out eventually.

"Do you know why we're here?"

I nodded. "Alice…it's her, isn't it?"

"Did you know her?" The male officer started writing something down in his notebook while the female asked me a lot of questions.

I told them everything I'd already said to Emma. I told them nothing at all.

They went away and promised they'd be in touch. They didn't arrest me. I thought they believed me, but I wasn't sure how long my story would hold up to close scrutiny. If Alice had told anyone about our trysts, I was in big trouble. They'd think I'd murdered her. They'd arrest me and my whole life would fall apart.

I paused at that thought. Would it be such a bad thing? The only negative I could think of would be the effect it might have on Ben. I didn't want him to get hurt. I didn't want him to grow up knowing I'd been fucking an eighteen year-old girl in my car while his mother was at home taking care of him.

When Emma came home I told her about the visit from the police.

"Shit," she said. "What will people think?"

There was no concern for me, nothing about the murdered girl. All that mattered was what her gaggle of yoga chums might make of it all.

Later, I went out and walked along to the park. She was there. She was always there. The red and white tape fencing her off from the public was loose. One of the metal poles was leaning over as if someone had pushed it. The tape flickered like a torn flag in the breeze. I went over there and put it right, straightening the post and leaning my weight against the top of it so it slid into its little hole in the concrete. I tied the tape around the pole and stepped away.

There was no one else around. She tended to draw a small crowd in daylight, but nobody came here after dark.

Occasionally busloads of tourists came to see her, mostly at weekends. They got off the bus, stood staring at her for a while, took a few photographs, bought some ice cream, and then went to a nearby pub for lunch. They usually got on the coach half-drunk and laughing about Dead Girl, barely even wondering what her constant reappearance might mean. To them, it was just a nice day out, a short trip to the dark side.

"I'm sorry," I said, but I didn't know why. There was nothing to apologise for. All I'd done was have sex with her. She'd seduced me, and I'd gone along with it in the hope it would make me feel less empty. But instead, it opened up the void at the centre of my life even wider. It was a harsh lesson. There was no sense of the numinous in adultery. Casual sex held no hidden spiritual significance, not to me.

Everything had stopped for her, but for me it just kept on changing.

I turned around and walked away, past the shut-up ice cream stand, the empty grassed areas, and towards the park entrance. I stood outside watching the main road. There wasn't much traffic. It would be difficult to get knocked down by a passing car at this time of the evening, when the after-work rush had died down. Not that I wanted to be run over, but it was something to think about before I went home.

I thought about killing Alice. If I had done it, would I have picked the same method as whoever had taken her as their victim? I didn't think so. It was too intimate; there was too much touching involved. I'd use a knife, or, better still, a gun. I had no idea where to get a gun, but that's what I'd choose. All you had to touch was the bullet. You could do it from yards away and pretend it was nothing to do with you.

And why did she keep on coming back? It felt like it might have something to do with me, but surely it was meant for her killer. Was she haunting him? Did she even know who he was? Or was she haunting the entire town, reminding us all of how frail everything is, how we should never forget we are rushing towards our own endings?

I crossed the road, walked along towards my street, and turned to face the park entrance. There was a figure standing there, outside the open gates, staring at me: a man, average height and build, wearing a pair of dark trousers and a lighter-coloured sports jacket. I raised a hand and waved at him.

He didn't wave back…

…I didn't wave back.

I stood outside the park gates watching the man who was standing at the end of my street, dressed exactly the same as me, and felt a massive sense of dislocation, as if time and space had stuttered for a second and I'd come loose from my own existence. I wasn't even sure where I was meant to be, here outside the park or over there at the end of my street. Or was I supposed to be in both places at once?

The man turned and walked away, along my street. I crossed the road and followed him. By the time I reached my front door, he was out of sight. I hadn't even seen him. He was a ghost of a ghost of me, lost for a moment on the treadmill of memory. He was something I wasn't meant to see.

#

"Did you ever really love me?" Emma was staring at me, her eyes blazing. We were in the kitchen. The air felt warm, as if someone was cooking. I had no idea how we'd got here, to this point. I couldn't remember the argument that had led to this accusation. It felt as if time were slipping, I was losing track. Lacunae were opening up in my consciousness and I kept falling through, finding myself somewhere else.

"Of course I did...I do. I love you. I love both of you." Did I mean her and Ben, or her and Alice – her and Dead Girl?

She threw her wine glass at the wall. The glass shattered; red wine spattered across the wallpaper, making a Rorschach ink blot pattern reminding me of something from my childhood, a dream, a memory, a small toy I'd once owned: perhaps a doll or a puppet. There was so much that I couldn't grasp. My past slipped away from me, skidding across the thin ice on the surface of my mind.

"I can't even reach you anymore. There's nobody there, nobody left inside you." I thought she might be about to cry.

I thought about the man I'd seen earlier that evening, the one who looked just like me. I wondered where he was now. Or was he actually here, going through this with me? What if I couldn't see him? Is your own ghost invisible to you most of the time? Is it even possible to haunt yourself?

"I'm sorry." I sat down at the table and clutched my hands, wringing them out as if they were wet. "I don't know anything anymore. Nothing makes sense. I don't know what to do." I pressed my hands down onto the table, wishing the wood or the bones would break. I didn't care which.

She started to pace, long strides across the kitchen. "You know what they're saying about you, don't you?"

"Who?"

She stopped pacing. "Everyone."

"No. I have no idea. What are they saying?"

Her smile was horrible, a wound put on display. "They say you were having an affair. That you were fucking her. Is that true? Were you *fucking* her?"

I shook my head. "I don't know."

"What the hell do you mean? How can you not know?" She stalked towards me on the other side of the table, clenching her fists. She was so angry spittle was gathering at the sides of her mouth.

"I don't think it was me. It was *him*...the other one. I think *he* was fucking her, but *I* can remember it. I was watching them."

She moved quicker than I'd thought possible. I didn't think she was even capable of such speed. She darted round to my side of the table, raised her fist, and punched me in the side of the face. I tipped sideways from the force of the blow, reaching out to grab the edge of the table so I didn't fall out of the chair. I didn't fight back. It wasn't worth it. She always won in the end.

"Bastard!" She left the room, slamming the door behind her. A minute later, I heard her crying. A short time after that, I heard her speaking to someone on the phone.

I didn't know what to do so I left through the rear door. I walked down to the end of the street, turned left, crossed the main road, and went into the park. The gates were never shut. You could access the park twenty-four hours a day. Sometimes kids would go in there late at night and make a racket, but mostly it was quiet. I looked up at the silent trees, breathed in the still, quiet air. The sky seemed to draw away from me, creating space. My body was light. I felt as if I could skip off the surface of the world.

I went down to the skate park and stood beside the ramp. I closed my eyes for a while. When I opened them again, he was there with her, lying at her side: my ghost, that other self. He was exactly like me. Same face, same eyes, same clothes. His eyes were open and he was looking at me, but there was no judgement in them. His mouth opened, his lips moved, but he didn't speak. There was nothing he could possibly say to put things right.

The plastic bag was still pulled tight over Alice's face. Nothing about her had changed. She was the only unchanging thing in a constantly shifting world. She was an anchor, something I could cling to as the universe mutated around me. I realised that now. I only wished I'd thought about it when she was alive. Then things might have been different. Perhaps he wouldn't have killed her.

I reached out and tore down the police tape, then entered the sanctity of the small area where Alice was laid to rest. There was a small gap between the two stiff bodies. It wasn't much, but there was just about enough room to manoeuvre. I reversed and forced myself between them, feeling the hard surface of the skate ramp pressing into my spine. I wriggled slightly so I was snuggled in tight with my hands crossed over my chest.

I stared up at the distant night sky, at the stars, and the gaps between the stars. I wondered if there were any answers there, floating around in the cosmos, just waiting to be found. I moved my hands away from my chest and put my arms down by my sides. I opened my hands. Waited.

Not long after that, I felt a cold, cold hand slip into each of mine. My body trembled; my palms began to sweat. The sky above me first loomed towards me and then pulled back again, opening up like a vast cosmic doorway. I closed my fingers. They squeezed my moist hands. Their skin was cold and as dry as bone.

Slowly, everything began to make sense.

I never wanted to let go. So when I stood and stepped up through that giant open doorway, I took them both with me. I loved them. I wanted them to share in whatever I was about to discover.

The following stories are original to this collection:

Trog Boy Ran
I Live in the Gut
You Haven't Seen Me
Hungry Love
Alice, Hanging Out in the Skate Park

The versions of all reprinted stories herein represent the author's preferred versions.

Story Notes:

Just Another Horror Story

I wrote this as a submission to Des Lewis's *The Horror Anthology of Horror Anthologies* project. It was the first short story I'd written for a while, and I was very pleased with the result. Des rejected the tale, but I felt that it was special and deserved a good home. Rather than send this elsewhere, I decided to hang on to it, and the story was one of the things that prompted the idea for this collection.

Barcode

This one was written in response to the global credit crunch, which then turned into the global recession we're still going through. There's not much more to say, I'm afraid. The story hopefully speaks for itself. Worth noting: this is probably the only story I've ever written that has a happy ending. I doubt the recession will have one.

The Row

The gorgeous Kahil Gibran quote at the beginning of this story inspired the whole thing. I love the notion of haunted people coming into contact, or colliding, with a haunted place, and the thought that sometimes, just sometimes, we are our own ghosts – and we are simply haunting ourselves.

When One Door Closes

Another response to the recession, when I kept hearing about friends who were made redundant and then struggled to find new jobs. The story is also a commentary on all kinds of industries (including publishing), where certain doors remain forever closed unless you know the right people.

The Chair

It began with me looking out of my bedroom window late one night to see an old kitchen chair on the footpath outside a neighbour's house. What was it doing there? Who had put it there, and why? Then, an image – perhaps from a dream later that same night – of a woman with henna tattoos made from darkness writhing on her arms. She was sitting in the same chair, stiff and silent, and something had just left her side

Truth Hurts

Obviously this one's about lies and liars, and about the

damage caused by those lies. I love taking a metaphor and making it literal. The horror genre is a great tool for doing that, and the results can often be startling. Personally, I think this is one of the bitterest stories I've ever written.

Down

Inspired by various visits to cave systems in my youth, this is a short, creepy homage to the great Ramsey Campbell. Nothing more, nothing less: just a scary little story that takes place in the dark

Sounds Weird

I wrote this one for an anthology and then forgot to submit it. I'm always doing things like that – I have a rubbish memory. Sound is an often underused effect in horror fiction, and I tried to address that shortcoming with this brief tale. Again, it's a very bitter piece, and the ending never fails to depress me. This is one of those stories of mine that affects me deeply, and I'm not too keen on the feelings of despair it invokes when I read it.

The Table

This one's a sequel to *The Chair*, of course. The characters wouldn't leave me alone; they had a lot more to tell. They still do. I have ideas for further stories in the sequence, titled *The Drawer* and *The Room*. Perhaps one day I'll even write them.

The Sheep

My wife and I spent a long weekend in Corbridge, Northumberland, ostensibly because we needed a break. The trip was also a good excuse for me to do some research on a novel I was writing, and she'd never before experienced the beauty of Hadrian's Wall. This story came out of that trip – it's based on feelings and ideas I had when we did a long hike in the rain. Most of what's written happened. The rest *could* happen.

Small Things

In modern life, we often forget about the tiny mechanisms that make our society work. The pleases and thank-yous, the small gestures and subtle indications, the admission that we actually see other people as human beings and not just two-dimensional characters in the film of our own lives. This might be what happens when all of that breaks down and we stop acknowledging even the smallest of charitable acts.

It Knows Where You Live

I needed a strong story to cap off this collection and felt that I already had the perfect title in place. This one examines a lot of themes that keep popping up in my short fiction, and it also embraces my love of cheap, tacky horror films. I just hope it doesn't know where *I* live…

Trog Boy Ran

This was written for a proposed anthology the publisher Angry Robot was planning to put out. The theme was to use the name of the publisher and come up with a story. I used an anagram. The anthology idea died a death, but I finished the story because I liked it. Another inspiration for this story was Mini Motorbike Man. Now, Mini Motorbike Man was an imaginary man on a tiny motorbike I'd imagine driving along at the side of the motorway during long car journeys in my childhood. He'd leap over bushes and fences like Steve McQueen in *The Great Escape*, and always accompanied me when we had to travel far.

I Live in the Gut

Another one that was originally intended for an anthology, but I didn't feel the finished story quite worked so I sent them something else instead (which was accepted). I went back to this one and did a few more drafts, teasing the story out. I think the end result is weird, creepy, and very sad. It's the newest story here, and I feel it represents the current direction of a lot of my fiction.

It Won't be Long Now

I wrote this for inclusion in a free eBook given away to regular readers by Michael Wilson at *This is Horror*, which is a review site for horror fans. I like the story a lot, and had every intention of including it in a collection so it might reach a wider audience.

You Haven't Seen me

This is Horror again. This time I wrote the first thousand words of a story for a competition, and those who entered had to finish it off. The prize was that the story be published on the website. My wife suggested I write an ending myself, so I could see how it compared with the winner. Ray Cluley – a very fine writer himself – won the competition, and I'm happy to say his ending was a lot different to mine. Keen-eyed readers will spot that this story takes place in the vicinity of the Concrete Grove.

The Grotto

When writer, editor and publisher Ian Whates asked me for a Christmas story to contribute to a promotional eBook aimed at potential and existing Newcon Press readers, I had no idea what to write. Then the title came into my head, followed by an image of a small boy struggling with family commitments and looking for someone – or some *thing* – to help him. After that, the story kind of wrote itself.

Hungry Love

I was asked to write a story for a gay-themed horror anthology, a follow-up to a book in which a story of mine had appeared previously. The title came quickly, as did the basic concept, but it took me a long time (and several rewrites) to find the narrative voice and the core of the story. I liked the idea that somebody's love could have a mind of its own, and it was a monster. It seemed funny and creepy, and I think the end result works well.

Alice, Hanging Out in the Skate Park

Somebody wrote these words in a Facebook update – I can't remember the context, but it struck me as a great title for a story, so I went away and wrote it. My friend Stephen Volk was involved in the Facebook thread, and I think it both amused and exasperated him when I told him what I'd done.

Gary McMahon is the acclaimed author of nine novels and several short story collections. His latest novel releases are BEYOND HERE LIES NOTHING (the third in the acclaimed Concrete Grove series, published by Solaris) THE END (an apocalyptic drama published by NewCon Press) and THE BONES OF YOU (a supernatural mystery published by Earthling Publications), and his short fiction has been reprinted in various "Year's Best" volumes.

Gary lives with his family in Yorkshire, where he trains in Shotokan karate and likes running in the rain.

Connect with Gary McMahon

Website: www.garymcmahon.com

Twitter: https://twitter.com/GaryMc_twatter

Connect with Crystal Lake Publishing

Website (be sure to sign up for our newsletter):
www.crystallakepub.com

Facebook:
www.facebook.com/Crystallakepublishing

Twitter:
https://twitter.com/crystallakepub

We hope you enjoyed this title. If so, we would be grateful if you could leave a review on Amazon, Goodreads, your blog or one of the many websites open to book reviews. Reviews are essential for a successful book. And remember to keep an eye out for more of our books. We have collections by Daniel I. Russell and Kevin Lucia, a novella by Paul Kane, as well as brilliant anthologies, with more amazing titles to come, including collections by William Meikle and Jasper Bark.

THANK YOU FOR PURCHASING THIS BOOK